PRAISE FOR

YOU CAN CROSS THE MASSACRE ON FOOT

Freddy Prestol Castillo's testimonial novel, *You Can Cross the Massacre on Foot*, is a key text in understanding the thirty-one-year dictatorship of Rafael Leonidas Trujillo and the little-known racist massacre that occurred in 1937, the slaughter of 10,000–40,000 Haitians who found themselves on the wrong side of the border. (The total is still under debate—as corpses cannot report on casualties, many of them thrown in the sea.) Had it not been for an American journalist, Quentin Reynolds, who reported on the massacre in *Collier's Magazine*, the world might not have known about this atrocity. Even so, international attention was focused on Europe and the rumors and rumbles of the oncoming war. The Trujillo regime repressed all reporting, so the massacre was never officially or sufficiently addressed or redressed.

Until the publication of Prestol Castillo's novel thirty-six years later, in 1973, no Dominican writer dared tackle this atrocity. The value of Prestol Castillo's book is its basis in the eyewitness reporting of the author, who at the time of the massacre was a judge stationed at the border. Troubling and eye-opening, the novel displays the origins of such genocides and the complicity of all those who remain silent. It's why the telling of the story is so important, as we consider the pervasive racism and violence toward others that persist throughout our hemisphere and within our own borders.

Margaret Randall turns her considerable talent and compassionate imagination to a translation of this work, continuing in the footsteps of Quentin Reynolds and her own trajectory as an author-translator-activist who has spent a lifetime giving voice to the silenced stories of our América. Her work has been instrumental in introducing many North American readers to our neighbors to the south, their history, literature, and struggles.

—JULIA ALVAREZ, author of *In the Time of the Butterflies*

A book in the series
LATIN AMERICA IN TRANSLATION /
EN TRADUCCIÓN / EM TRADUÇÃO
*Sponsored by the Duke–University of North Carolina
Program in Latin American Studies*

YOU CAN CROSS THE MASSACRE ON FOOT

TRANSLATED BY MARGARET RANDALL
AND WITH A FOREWORD BY MARIA CRISTINA FUMAGALLI

FREDDY PRESTOL CASTILLO

Duke University Press   Durham and London   2019

© 2019 Duke University Press. Original Spanish © 1998 Ediciones de TALLER
All rights reserved. Designed by Courtney Leigh Baker and typeset in Garamond
Premier Pro and Century Schoolbook by Westchester Publishing Services.

Library of Congress Cataloging-in-Publication Data
Names: Prestol Castillo, Freddy, author. | Randall, Margaret, [date] translator. |
Fumagalli, Maria Cristina, writer of supplementary text.
Title: You can cross the massacre on foot / Freddy Prestol Castillo ;
translated by Margaret Randall ; and with a foreword by Maria Cristina Fumagalli. Other
titles: Masacre se pasa a pie. English
Description: Durham : Duke University Press, 2019. |
Series: Latin America in translation/en traducciâon/em traducao |
Includes bibliographical references and index.
Identifiers: LCCN 2018044277 (print)
LCCN 2018049807 (ebook)
ISBN 9781478004448 (ebook)
ISBN 9781478003205 (hardcover)
ISBN 9781478003830 (pbk.)
Subjects: LCSH: Dominican Republic—History—1930–1961—Fiction. |
Dominican-Haitian Conflict, 1937—Fiction. | LCGFT: Fiction.
Classification: LCC PQ7409.2.P7 (ebook) |
LCC PQ7409.2.P7 M313 2019 (print) | DDC 863/.62—dc23
LC recordavailableat https:// lccn.loc.gov/2018044277

Cover art: © Solange Paradis. Ouanaminthe, Haiti.
January 2009. Courtesy of the artist.

The book you are about to read chronicles, primarily, the 1937 mass-acre of Haitians and Haitian Dominicans carried out by the army of the Dominican dictator Rafael Leonidas Trujillo. The Massacre River, living up to its name, became one of the bloodiest sites in the onslaught.

Initially colonized by the Spanish who arrived on the island in 1492, Hispaniola became contested territory when the French slowly began to invade the northern side of the island in the seventeenth century. In his *Description topographique, physique, civile, politique et historique de la partie française de l'isle Saint-Domingue* (1797), Mé-déric Louis Élie Moreau de Saint-Méry explains that the Massacre River owes its name to "ancient murderous acts reciprocally commit-ted by the Buccaneers and the Spaniards in their disputes over the territory."[1] Saint-Méry, however, is cautious not to highlight the fact that the French had de facto occupied a portion of the island: more precisely, in fact, the Massacre River was named after the slaughter of a company of French boucaniers and border trespassers killed by the Spanish in 1728, when the island was still officially a Spanish colony.

In his *Description topographique et politique de la partie espagnole de l'isle Saint-Domingue* (1796), Saint-Méry includes an *Abrégé histo-rique*, a historical summary which records the history of Hispaniola's colonial border between Spain and France up to 1777, when the two nations signed the Treaty of Aranjuez that legitimized the French occupation of the island. According to the treaty, the border begins with the d'Ajabon, or Massacre River, in the north of the island and ends with the Anse à Pitre, or Pedernales River, in the south.[2]

The Treaty of Aranjuez and Saint-Méry's comment cast the line of demarcation between the two colonies, on which the events at the core of Freddy Prestol Castillo's *El Masacre se pasa a pie* unfold, as a "natural" border that had traditionally been the theater of conflict and violence. Yet the title of Prestol Castillo's book reminds us that "the Massacre can be crossed on foot," implicitly introducing us to a porous border where the two peoples could easily engage in exchanges and form collaborative linkages.

The 1937 massacre of Haitians and Haitian Dominicans in the northern provinces of the Dominican Republic is generally referred to as *el Corte* (the Cutting) by Dominicans and as *kout kouto-a* (the stabbing) by Haitians because it was mostly carried out with machetes and knives in order to make it look like a popular insurrection against Haitians who were accused of stealing livestock. The killings began on September 28, 1937; intensified on October 2; and lasted until October 8, with sporadic murders continuing until November 5.[3] The estimated number of victims is still disputed and ranges from 10,000 to 40,000; for the most part they were small farmers who had lived in the Dominican Republic for generations or who were even born there and therefore were in fact Dominican citizens, since until 2010 the Dominican constitution granted citizenship on the basis of ius soli.[4]

The idea that the massacre might have been a reaction to Haitians crossing the border to steal has now been discarded as an after-the-fact fabrication, but there is still a fair amount of debate surrounding the causes of the massacre.[5] At the time, the Dominican and Haitian central governments did not have much control of the borderland and the border had been finalized only a year earlier as Trujillo and the Haitian president Sténio Vincent, encouraged by the United States, had signed additional clauses to a 1929 border agreement. Despite laws that aimed to make border crossings more difficult, people continued to circulate more or less freely between the two countries, and migration from Haiti to the Dominican Republic continued, relatively undisturbed.[6] The Dominican historian Bernardo Vega has argued that in 1935, after the return to Haiti of tens of thousands of braceros who had been expelled from Cuba, the Haitian presence in the area substantially increased, creating social, political, and racial tensions. One of the main factors that caused the massacre, Vega insists, was the desire of the Dominican ruling classes to "whiten" their nation.[7] Lauren Derby and Richard Turits argue instead that the real aim of the massacre was to destroy the frontier's bicultural, bilingual, and transnational Haitian Dominican communities.[8] As Turits has eloquently put it, in fact, the 1937 massacre is also a story of "Dominicans versus Dominicans, Dominican elites versus Dominican peasants, the national state against Dominicans in the frontier, centralizing forces in opposition to local interests, and, following the massacre, the newly hegemonic anti-Haitian discourses of the nation vying with more culturally pluralist discourses and memories from the past."[9]

In *El Masacre se pasa a pie*, victims and perpetrators are often related, have strong bonds of affection, or clearly depend on each other for their livelihood: Captain Ventarrón, who has been ordered to slaughter not only men but also old people, women, and children, suddenly remembers that his grandfather was born in Haiti and manages to continue with his horrific task only by getting increasingly drunk.[10] Sargent Pío's illegitimate sister had married the Haitian Yosefo Dis, a wealthy owner of crops and cattle who had lived for twenty years in the Dominican Republic, considered himself Dominican, and was in possession of official documents that legitimized his status. Yosefo and his Dominican wife had seven children, and Pío, who is one of the military men in charge of the killings, lets them escape to Haiti instead of slaughtering them: as he looks to his sister going to a country she doesn't know and thinks about her children, destined to live among people who speak a language they do not know, Pío looks like a condemned man. Mistress Francina, the innkeeper of Dajabón and a member of the town's elite, lies and risks her life in order to hide and help Moraime Luis, one of her workers who had grown up with her, who was baptized in Dajabón in Spanish, and who considered the Dominican Republic her own country: when she is captured, raped, and, eventually, killed on the bank of the river, Moraime screams (crucially) in two languages. Don Sebusto, a landowner whose land and cattle, due to *el Corte*, are going to be left unattended, voices his worries about the financial loss that the elimination of the "Haitian" workforce will cause him (46).

The 1937 massacre, as we have seen, was perpetrated mostly by Trujillo's army, and Dominican civilians responded in different ways to it. As Prestol Castillo shows, Francina is not the only Dominican who exposes herself to danger by hiding "Haitian" friends or relatives and helping them flee the soldiers. Others, however, usually civil local authorities loyal to Trujillo, collaborated with the regime, locating and identifying "Haitians" for the guards.[11] Some civilians were given the task of burying and burning the corpses, but it appears that, generally, they did not take an active part in the massacre, with the exception of prisoners recruited in Dominican jails and the destitute *reservistas* who were promised freedom and land for their services or were simply obliged to become assassins to save their own lives. The narrator calls them *obreros del crimen* (53) and points out that while some were callous murderers who had no problem with the atrocities they were asked to commit and were ready to take advantage of the situation to help themselves to the properties of their victims, others found it extremely difficult to participate in the killings and to cope with the pressure and the violence they were forced to witness and take part in. Some were executed for refusing to kill, and the many who lost their minds or were turned into desperate alcoholics by the experience are presented as victims of the dictatorship, which—not unproblematically, of course—is what is ultimately blamed for *el Corte*.

Apart from offering an important insight into the massacre, the multiethnic nature of the borderland, and the mechanics of Trujillo's violent and oppressive regime, Prestol Castillo's book also reveals how, due to the Dominican Republic's proximity to Haiti, the Dominican elite of the time regarded the borderland (at best) as a series of half-civilized outposts: when the narrator first heard the name

"Dajabón" at school, during geography lesson, it was pronounced by a teacher who read the *Times*, had never visited the borderland, and had assumed that Dajabón and the nearby villages were uninteresting, unbearable, unpleasant, the opposite of everything he regarded as civilization (17). As a child the narrator was intrigued by the name, but as a young man he accepted to move to Dajabón very reluctantly and only because his landowning sugar family had lost its fortune and he could not find a better job; despite what seems a sympathetic approach to its inhabitants, the condescension with which he regards them and what he calls their "little peasant's brains" is unmistakable (133).

Arguably, it was the publication of Edwidge Danticat's award-winning *The Farming of Bones* in 1998, followed by the 1999 translation into English of Jacques Stephen Alexis's *Compère général soleil* (1955) and, in 2005, of René Philoctète's *Le peuple des terres mêlées* (1989), that greatly contributed to raise awareness, in the Anglophone world, about the 1937 massacre. These three texts differ in style but share important features: they are all fictional accounts, written years after the massacre, and while Philoctète and Alexis are Haitian writers, Danticat is a member of the Haitian diaspora in the United States. Danticat's book, however, is written as if it were a first-person account or *testimonio*: this immediacy of tone has been identified as one of the reasons for its success. *El Masacre se pasa a pie*, instead, was written by a Dominican author who offers it as a personal account of the massacre by an eyewitness who was commenting on the facts as they unfolded in front of his eyes. Initially drafted in 1937, during Prestol Castillo's stay in Dajabón, the book was not published until thirty-six years after the massacre and twelve years after Trujillo's assassination, for fear of retaliation. To begin with, the manuscript was entrusted to "Doctor M" (9); retrieved from his office by a priest when the doctor was arrested by the "Secret Service" (11), it was sent to the author only years later. Hidden by the author's mother and later buried by his sister in the family garden, the manuscript was finally dug up in poor condition, with torn pages, almost illegible in parts, and Prestol Castillo had to painstakingly reconstruct it. When it was published in 1973, *El Masacre se pasa a pie* sold twenty thousand copies in a relatively short time and also became required reading in Dominican schools: its success can be explained, at least in part, by the fact that it tries to address, albeit in contradictory and sometimes controversial ways, the sense of guilt Dominicans might have felt and still feel about the massacre.

Stylistically, *El Masacre se pasa a pie* is not a polished work, but it can be argued that this only lends further poignancy to its content and that its little regard for structure and its chaotic nature mirror the urgency of the situation during the problematic times in which Prestol Castillo was living.[12] The author's presence is felt more palpably in the first and last parts of the book, where we are also presented with his love interest and one of the most striking figures of the novel, Angela Vargas. Angela is a young teacher from Azua who was sent to work in a school in the borderland, and she risks her life to protect her students during *el Corte*. Through Angela, the book also sheds light on the regime's gender politics and on its systemic sexual exploitation of Dominican women. Angela, however, refuses to succumb to the demands and threats of those who want to take advantage of her poverty, and, finally, she decides to leave the country in order to live her life with dignity and in freedom. In his preface, Prestol Castillo discloses that, like his narrator, he was repeatedly and forcefully exhorted to leave by his own fiancée, a schoolteacher who had already fled the country: it is perhaps as a tribute to the courage of this *guerrillera* (and, implicitly, to the courage of Prestol Castillo's mother and sister, who had refused to destroy his manuscript despite the danger they were facing by keeping it) that the narrator gives his own notes on *el Corte* not to a male friend but to Angela, whom he considers smart and valiant enough to guard what he describes as the equivalent of a "time bomb" (177).

The central section of *El Masacre se pasa a pie* can be seen instead as a series of sketches where the author seems to be reporting, verbatim (often reproducing local speech), dialogues between soldiers, victims, and local landowners that, however, he is unlikely to have actually heard. The distinction between facts and fiction, autobiography and novel, in fact, is intriguingly blurred in this book. As we have seen, like his narrator, Prestol Castillo arrived to work as a magistrate in the border town of Dajabón during the massacre itself, and *El Masacre se pasa a pie* presents us with the point of view of someone observing the unfolding tragedy but who is imbricated—albeit reluctantly—with the Dominican regime. The narrator repeatedly calls himself a coward and even refers to himself as a *testigo cómplice*, that is, an eyewitness who is also an accomplice to the crimes he directly observes, for not speaking up against the atrocities (173).[13] It is possible that Prestol Castillo wrote this manuscript at the same time in which, in his capacity as a judge, he was producing "accounts" of the massacre that were more in line with the official version of the facts that the regime was keen to circulate. *El Masacre se pasa a pie*, therefore, could be seen as the product of a conscience tortured by guilt and regret for not joining the many exiled intellectuals that the regime could not silence or pay off. In *Paisajes y meditaciones de una frontera* ("Landscapes of and meditations on the frontier"), published in 1943, for example, Prestol Castillo never mentions the 1937 massacre, but Trujillo (the volume's dedicatee) is repeatedly praised for having "improved" the situation on the borderland of the Dominican Republic, an area of the country Prestol Castillo claims was in desperate need of being claimed back by the state.[14] At the same time, however, while in Dajabón, Prestol Castillo painstakingly recorded compromising facts and impressions, clandestinely producing a manuscript that might have cost him his life had it been found by Trujillo's secret police. Yet, like his narrator, who entrusts his own manuscript to friends and relatives for safekeeping, Prestol Castillo never took the decision to destroy this potentially explosive and incriminating work.

The author's deep anxiety and his inability and unwillingness to either fully embrace or resolutely reject the regime and its dominant discourses are evident in the text's many contradictions. Racist, xenophobic, and elitist prejudices abound: Haitians are described as a "primitive race" (95), but at the same time, the narrator is shocked and profoundly shaken by the violence perpetrated against them. In line with the regime's propaganda, the narrator refers to "Haitians" as thieves who come in the night to steal cattle; however, the story of Don Francisco, whose land straddled the frontier, offers a different perspective on the situation and sheds light on the hypocrisy of the landholding class. Before the massacre, when some of his cattle were stolen, Don Francisco was not too concerned because he knew that he would still make a huge profit with the low salary he was paying those who worked for (and occasionally stole from) him in order to support themselves and their families; like other local landowners, Don Francisco used instead to routinely curse taxes and other measures that hampered his profitable trade with the neighboring country. However, when his property is visited by the army engaged in *el Corte*, he vociferously complains only about the "Haitians" and their stealing.

In Prestol Castillo's text, Haitian thieving appears to have ruined some Dominican families who had members in the army who were particularly keen to take part in the massacre in order to take revenge against those they considered responsible for their change of fortune and diminished circumstances. The narrator, however, also reveals that the "Haitians" mostly returned in the night to steal the produce they had grown on Dominican land for years, or came to take the livestock they had long nurtured as if it were part of their own family, showing that, in fact, some of the thievery at least took place after the massacre. The narrator also points out that, after *el Corte*, those who had left everything behind when they found refuge in Haiti had no choice but to turn to criminality and to enter into the Dominican Republic illegally to steal cattle or other produce in order to feed themselves and their starving children: while the narrator seems genuinely sympathetic and troubled about their suffering, the idea of more and more "hungry Haitians" crossing the border to steal from Dominicans (101) chimes with anti-Haitian discourses that depict the Dominican Republic as a nation threatened by a possible "invasion" of the disenfranchised poor of the neighboring country. At the same time, however, the narrator seems to suggests that these border crossers were somehow entitled to reclaim the fruit of their labor and goes as far as wondering to whom the land really belonged (88): to the "Haitians," who had transformed it into orchards, or to those Dominicans who had left it uncultivated before 1937 and would continue to do so after *el Corte*? After the massacre, the narrator continues, Dominicans re-cruited in Santo Domingo's underbelly, or destitute people who had been declared "vagrants" because they owned no land, were brought to the borderland in army trucks to substitute the workers who had been slaughtered. The difference between these new arrivals and the Haitians and Haitian Dominicans who cultivated the land and made it productive was very striking: they were neither keen nor able to work and only longed to go back to the city. As a result, he explains, a year after their arrival, most of the new arrivals were sent back to the capital, poorer than when they had arrived.

El Masacre se pasa a pie also reveals how the Dominicans' collective unconscious was deeply affected by nationalistic discourses that identified Haitians as cruel and savage invaders and perpetrators of horrific violence. During a delirious night, the narrator, feverish and deeply distressed by *el Corte*, has a nightmare during which he is "vis-ited" by Toussaint Louverture, who professes that he will kill all the inhabitants of the Spanish side. Jean-Jacques Dessalines and Emperor Faustin Soulouque also appear to him in a bloodbath in which fierce Haitian *caníbales* (181) destroy churches and slaughter both whites and blacks from Santo Domingo. This account ends with the narrator pondering the history of the crimes committed by the Haitians that he had learned at school when he was a child—for example, the trail of death and destruction left by the Haitian army led by Dessalines and Henri Christophe, the abuses committed by Jean-Pierre Boyer during the unification of the island (1822–44), and the policy of aggression orchestrated by Soulouque in 1849 and 1855—and, simultaneously, the present history, equally written in blood, that was unfolding in front of him. We are not told what conclusions the narrator draws from his meditation, but the mere contraposition and comparison be-tween Dominican and Haitian brutality explodes the received notion that barbarism, cruelty, savagism, and ferocity pertained only to one side of the border.

El Masacre se pasa a pie also identifies Haitians with black magic: we are informed, in fact, that they resorted to supernatural assistance to secure protection. A case in point is the story of El Patú, a desperate father and cunning cattle thief who solicited the help of a powerful *bocó*, or sorcerer, to avoid capture (95). However, when, after losing his mind and agonizing for fourteen nights, the callous Dominican executioner El Panchito finally dies, the narrator explains that the people who witnessed his death saw four green snakes coming out of his mouth speaking Haitian "Patois," suggesting that they believed that his victims had somehow returned and possessed his body out of revenge for his cruelty (182). These stories show that Dominicans strongly credited and deeply feared the power of Haitian magic but also highlight that the two peoples shared the same system of belief, even if Haitians seem to have had what Derby has called the "monopoly of the sacred."[15]

After the massacre, as Prestol Castillo illustrates, the northern province of Dajabón and the nearby city of Montecristi became the stage for what has been called *el gran teatro* (the great theater).[16] It was there, in fact, that, in order to be seen to be responding to international pressure, the regime staged the trials and imprisonment of some of the (alleged) civilian perpetrators of the massacre. For that purpose, the *alcaldes pedáneos* (submunicipal political authorities) of the sites where the killings had taken place were ordered to select four or five reservists or "friends of Trujillo"; these young men were then taken to the prison of Montecristi and photographed dressed as convicts.[17] During the trials, they were given clear instructions on what to say or, as Prestol Castillo's narrator reveals, they were even provided with depositions prepared *ad hoc* by the judges themselves. Prestol Castillo's narrator makes it all too clear that, far from establishing the inconvenient truth, the job of the judges was to distort it and to fabricate convenient lies in order to corroborate the idea that the killings sprung from a spontaneous insurrection of Dominicans against Haitians. The web of deceit that the Dominican judges sent to the border to investigate *el Corte* were forced to spin, the narrator adds, took its toll on some of them: one tried to kill himself, another became an alcoholic, and a third escaped but was later arrested by the secret police and put in jail. Those judges who complied without complaining or experiencing a nervous breakdown were later betrayed by the system: they hoped for a reward but were instead sent home unceremoniously.[18]

El Masacre se pasa a pie ends in a rather abrupt way after our attention is refocused on the narrator, who, after having escaped from Dajabón, is pursued by the police and agonizes about whether he should leave the country or remain to support his family. When he finally decides to flee, hidden in a boat headed to Venezuela, he is captured by the coast guard because, in an ironic twist, he once again finds himself implicated in another atrocity—which, however, receives very little attention in the book—namely, the throwing overboard of a group of clandestine Chinese by a member of the crew who had robbed them, killed them, and then fed them to the sharks. Falsely accused by a terrified and subservient judge, the narrator is condemned to five years in prison: at that point, however, we know that his manuscript is safe with his mother, to whom it was dutifully delivered by Angela Vargas before her departure.

Arguably, reading *El Masacre se pasa a pie* can occasionally be a disturbing experience and not only because it describes a ruthless massacre. Its old-fashioned, frequently gauche, prose and its chaotic structure, in fact, present us with an equally frenzied and disorganized attempt to come to terms with personal and collective guilt and the simultaneous urges to comprehend the causes of the killings, denounce or justify its perpetrators, and commemorate or blame its victims. It is a book that often frustrates its readers and can even make them feel uncomfortable at times. However, this does not make it any less compelling.

NOTES

1. Médéric Louis Élie Moreau de Saint-Méry, *Description topographique, physique, civile, politique et historique de la partie française de l'isle Saint-Domingue. Avec des observations générales sur la population, sur le caractère & les moeurs de ses divers habitans; sur son climat, sa culture, ses productions, son administrations &c, &c. accompagnées des détails les plus propres à faire connaître l'état de cette colonie à l'époque du 18 Octobre 1789; Et d'une nouvelle carte de la totalité de l'isle*, 2 vols. (Philadelphia: chez l'auteur, 1797–98), vol. 1, 108 (translation mine).

2. Médéric Louis Élie Moreau de Saint-Méry, *Description topographique et politique de la partie espagnole de l'isle Saint-Domingue. Avec des observations générales sur le climat, la population, les productions, le caractère & les moeurs des habitans de cette colonie et un tableau raisonné des différents parties de son administration; accompagnée d'une nouvelle carte de la totalité de l'isle,* 2 vols. (Philadelphia: chez l'auteur, 1796), vol. 1, i–xxii.

3. Bernardo Vega, *Trujillo y Haití,* 3 vols. (Santo Domingo: Fundación Cultural Dominicana, 1988–2009), vol. 2, 39.

4. Vega, *Trujillo y Haití,* vol. 2, 352–53; Richard Lee Turits, "A World Destroyed, a Nation Imposed: The 1937 Haitian Massacre in the Dominican Republic," *Hispanic American Historical Review* 82, no. 3 (2002): 590.

5. Vega, *Trujillo y Haití,* vol. 2, 33, 39; vol. 1, 323.

6. Samuel Martínez, *Peripheral Migrants: Haitians and Dominican Republic Sugar Plantations* (Knoxville: University of Tennessee Press, 1995), 44; Lauren Derby and Richard Turits, "Temwayaj Kout Kouto, 1937 / Eyewitness to the Genocide," in *Revolutionary Freedoms: A History of Survival, Strength and Imagination in Haiti,* ed. C. Accilien, J. Adams, and E. Méléance (Coconut Creek, FL: Caribbean Studies Press, 2006), 137–43; Turits, "A World Destroyed"; Lauren Derby, "Haitians, Magic, and Money: *Raza* and Society in the Haitian-Dominican Borderlands, 1900 to 1937," *Comparative Studies in Society and History* 36, no. 3 (1994): 488–526.

7. Vega, *Trujillo y Haití,* vol. 2, 343–44, 23–26.

8. Turits, "A World Destroyed"; Derby, "Haitians, Magic, and Money"; Derby and Turits, "Temwayaj Kout Kouto, 1937." Derby and Turits's findings were further confirmed by Edward Paulino, who, like them, also conducted a series of interviews with eyewitnesses of the massacre. See Edward Paulino, *Dividing Hispaniola: The Dominican Republic's Border Campaign against Haiti, 1930–1961* (Pittsburgh, PA: University of Pittsburgh Press, 2015), 56–83.

9. Turits, "A World Destroyed," 593.

10. Freddy Prestol Castillo, *El Masacre se pasa a pie* (Santo Domingo: Editora Taller, 1973). Hereafter, page references to this edition are given in parentheses in the text; translations from Spanish are mine.

11. The victims are generally identified collectively as "Haitians" even if the book makes it clear that many were Dominican citizens of Haitian descent or long-term residents who considered themselves Dominicans and had never been to Haiti.

12. For literary analysis in English of *El Masacre se pasa a pie,* see, among other books, Doris Somner, *One Master for Another: Populism as Patriarchal Rhetoric in Dominican Novels* (Lanham, MD: University Press of America, 1983), chapter 5; Jean Franco, *Cruel Modernity* (Durham, NC: Duke University Press, 2013), chap-

ter 1; Maria Cristina Fumagalli, *On the Edge: Writing the Border between Haiti and the Dominican Republic* (Liverpool: Liverpool University Press, 2015), chapter 5; Lorgia García-Peña, *The Borders of Dominicanidad: Race, Nation, and Archives of Contradiction* (Durham, NC: Duke University Press, 2016), chapter 3.

13. Presto Castillo himself pointed out in an interview with Doris Somner that the circumstances of the narrator's escape and imprisonment were the only part of *El Masacre se pasa a pie* that were not autobiographical (Somner, *One Master for Another*, 190).

14. Freddy Prestol Castillo, *Paisajes y meditaciones de una frontera* (Ciudad Trujillo: Editorial Cosmopolita, 1943), 63.

15. Derby, "Haitians, Magic, and Money," 517.

16. Rafael Darío Herrera, *Montecristi entre campeches y bananos* (Santo Domingo: Editora Búho, 2006), 139.

17. Herrera, *Montecristi entre campeches y bananos*, 139–40.

18. Most likely, the narrator—and, crucially, Prestol Castillo himself—was one of these judges, even if the book does not make this absolutely clear.

STORY OF A HISTORY

I wrote alone, beneath the border sky. I was in exile without knowing it. Although I wasn't locked up, in that wasteland it was clear enough that I was just another prisoner. Late at night I heard the endless howling of stray dogs, weightless like dry leaves, hungry, elastic like the hacienda's nooses. I wrote furtively, while the village slept. And in that deep meander of silence I pondered my sad fate: condemned to loneliness, like all my generation punished into silence. Each night I left the shack and gazed at the border night. Such beautiful stars. And then that sky, dense and low, seemed to smother me. In the intimacy of that moment a single word came to me: loneliness. It was a word filled with horror.

At night, by the light of a flickering yellow beeswax tallow candle, I read. Then I told myself: "I've gained in root what I've lost in leaves!"

I said it out loud, as if in protest or as a description of my life.

I felt comforted.

The village nights were heavy with dagger wounds, with freed prisoners. The night smelled of rum.

Alone, in that sad hut, surrounded by darkness, an accusatory inner voice whispered: "Coward! Get out!" The voice continued until dawn, when sleep overtook me.

Yes, I should have fled. I should be free. I should have forsaken passivity and hidden in a fisherman's sloop. Instead, I had succumbed to capture in exchange for the piece of bitter bread I gave my mother.

The letters from my lady friend, a schoolteacher who had managed to flee the country, repeated the same plea: Leave. Go in search of freedom! Instead, I remained in town like an ox yoked to a plow. I thought of the randomness of the days to come. Time passed but seemed to have come to a stop. Gray days, one like the next, the color of the grass that surrounded the village, that savannah that seemed like a stepmother, in whose solitary extension my thoughts roamed.

THIS IS WHAT TYRANNY IS. Tyranny has a face like a statue: it never laughs. Tyranny strangles you with its dangerous yellow gaze. (Each time I sat down to write, the yellow eyes of tyranny would stare up at me from the paper.)

Tyranny is the tyrant and also everyone who is not the tyrant. Tyranny is Don Panchito, the killer—he who would agonize for fourteen nights, crowing like a rooster, croaking like a frog, snorting like a pig.

Corporal Sugilio too: pincer hands, the deep-set eyes of a caged animal, a leopard's demeanor. Don Panchito, the killer, and Corporal Sugilio would be everywhere. Didn't they try to find my book? Didn't they spy on my writing? Ah, no. Don Panchito can't read! Neither can Corporal Sugilio. It's safe for me to write at night!

FOR ALL MY SUFFERING, I'd finished my book. If it had fallen into the hands of the secret police, I would have been condemned to death.

Danger turned me and my book into two oppressed beings. One day I escaped the town. From that moment on, the book had its own biography.

In the book's biography is the story of Doctor M and Father Oscar. The latter owes his life to these pages. I owe mine to them too. Here I will briefly tell you the story of the doctor and Father Oscar.

The doctor was a man of wisdom and human sensibility. He had a profound knowledge of this magical island, its rivers, its mountains, its history and people. He could speak for hours about the Dominican man, from the time of Columbus's landing aboard The Isabella. He could also tell you about all the species of the island's insects, birds, and fish. He was an exquisite conversationalist: volatile, a miracle worker, a mulatto Don Quixote. At times, he seemed deranged. But always brilliant and brave. At the university, his classes in medicine drew all sorts of students, even those from other disciplines. In the late afternoon, the doctor's lectures, uttered in a voice as soft as a soliloquy, attracted students from the School of Law. Sometimes those lectures were like slow rain, and at others like savage torrents. The digressions with which he enlivened them were marvelous. In short, a genius of a man! A well-known surgeon, clinician, botanist, novelist, speaker, researcher, troublemaker. He was asphyxiated by the tyranny's toxic atmosphere. Finally, suspect in the eyes of the dictatorship, we believed that at any moment, recklessly and under the cover of night, a paid assassin would put an end to his life as he exited his classroom or simply lingered on any corner.

I had entrusted him with the original of my manuscript. He received it like something precious, eager to devour the scribbled text. I told him I wanted to copy it first, so he could read it more easily. He said no. He wanted to read it just as it had emerged from my mind.

IN HIS PRIVATE OFFICE on the outskirts of the capital, the doctor read the manuscript enthusiastically. From time to time he stopped reading and muttered to himself, interjecting opposing ideas, as if in discussion.

"What the devil!" he shouted.

"Goddamned country! . . . No, no, goddamned politicians! Because this is a poor and ignorant country, punished by hunger!

"Horror of horrors! Must we also repay debts of blood with blood? . . . No! Despite their last century's crimes, the Haitians are our most afflicted brothers, more afflicted even than we are.

"Goddamn dictatorship, destroying character and debasing men! Goddamned dictatorship . . . !"

Then he would fall silent again, walk in circles, pushing his spectacles back up on his nose and toying with his pointed moustache. All the while, *night fell around him. Crickets began to sing. And in the distance, the nightly voices of the mule drivers, hauling their loads of coal. From time to time he went to the high window as he read, catching a whiff of wild merengue or the far-off sound of midnight drums, tremulous and adulterated. The doctor stopped reading and said:*

"Yes . . . ! Yes . . . ! Woe to us . . . ! Woe to us . . . ! Poor little creatures that we are . . . ! Rum, drumbeat, merengue . . . and dictators . . . ! What use are our deep blue evenings, those brilliant stars, this scent of night as deep as the bark of a dog in the countryside? All this beauty? For what . . . ? Just so we may bear witness to barbary . . . ! Ah, yes . . . the Haitians, poor things. . . . They need sanitation, food, education. . . . Savages . . . ? Not unlike ourselves!" And he would exclaim:

"Damn . . . !

"When will we become human . . . ?"

A bell rang. The old housekeeper knocked at his door.

A violent mob—Secret Service hounds—entered the residence where there dwelt a silence like that which resides in colonial churches on days with neither rites nor faithful, those profound moments in old churches as evening approaches. The killers came with their arrogance. They were delinquents in the service of repression, bottom-feeding sons without fathers or teachers or bread. Only curse words and mud. They proliferate like yellow flowers in garbage dumps. They came with their histrionics and their hunger, like wild dogs. And they too are dogs. They went right from being children to being men. They've roamed with neither purpose nor bread. Of course, their business is crime. In local gangs (thieves persecuted by the police). Also thieves in military uniforms and with all the authority invested in them. Hounds, like wild dogs. But that is the price of their bread. Bread veined through and through with drops of blood. Without even the consent of judges.

"Where is that man? Where is he?"

The old housekeeper trembled.

Hoarse mule-driver voices, good for running cattle like those I used to hear in my childhood on the haciendas in the east. Voices good for frightening cattle and men blurred in the immensity of pastures and fields. And those mule-drivers' hands: large, worn, good for grabbing the head of a strong and savage bull, capable of quickly roping unruly and dangerous animals. A single toss of the rope and the bull is completely subjugated. Rough hands with which to crack the cattle whip at dusk. Corporal Sugilio roped cattle well but shouted at them even better. Now he'd forgotten all that. He'd also forgotten the art of controlling the plow handle and lifting the blade when it got caught in roots. Now he was a policeman, a hound. His boss paid him a miserable wage. It was like that for many of those from the countryside who would never plant again. The others, those from the city, don't even know the plow.

I digress as I remember the attack on the doctor. And I continue to digress. The evildoers' hands remind me of Doctor M's strong and colorful words in our talks. He would say:

"There won't be any chickens left on this earth . . . ! Those who should be planting corn are slack-mouthed in the parks and plazas, hungry, waiting for a chance to enroll in the army or become members of the Secret Service so they can kill . . . !"

The old housekeeper trembled. Horrified, she saw those clawlike hands going after the doctor. (The idler has a profession now; he is a detective.)

A hall door opened violently.

"Here I am!" (The doctor spoke with dignity.)

"Come on in!"

Corporal Sugilio: "Cuff him!" (Corporal Sugilio: A leopard. A cat. A vulture. A bird of prey. Red eyes, like those lights on the nearby television tower. He smells of rum. He fastens the handcuffs with astonishing speed.)

"Come on! Hurry up!"

The doctor spoke without losing his composure, arrogantly, contemptuously, calmly. Why was he so calm? Later we learned why. When he left the house, guarded by criminals, he had already decided to commit suicide in protest of the regime. (Before leaving his office, he looked down one last time at my book. It seemed as if even then, in that final instant, he was still contemplating a word or an image.)

Suddenly, one of the group penetrated the office. He must have been the leader of that mob. He took my book's original manuscript in his hands. Did he know how to read . . . ? Eager for blood, what did that mastiff want? His ignorance denied him another victim, me! Finally, he threw the pile of papers back on the doctor's desk. The book remained open, on the table, like a prostrated and lifeless beggar. The ruffian looked around. Only books . . . ! What a shame, he thought. He searched every corner of the room. Only books . . . ! Then he picked up the doctor's fine watch he noticed sitting beside those papers.

A few hours later the city learned of the incident. The famous Doctor M had tried to commit suicide. Using a razor blade, and with surgical precision, he'd traced a line across his throat. They found him passed out in the colonial tower that serves as the prison. They rescued him and took him to the state's best hospital. The owner of the nation "had lamented it all" (according to the press), and ordered that the doctor "be saved."

In that situation, no one dared visit the doctor's stately and silent home, where his natural history museum, his library, the unpublished books he'd written, and that good and awkward housekeeper so like an old wall clock weary of time, remained. The housekeeper trembled, mute after what she had just witnessed. And upon the table, my original book manuscript, open!

FATHER OSCAR—HIS FRIEND, his priest, a humanist and brilliant intellectual, a man of great virtue—entered the room. He wanted to restore order. He was intrigued by that pile of papers. Immediately he saw it was an unpublished book. With his insatiable reader's curiosity, he began to read. Astonishment flooded his countenance, and he bent over the papers in earnest. As he read, his face registered profound emotion. Those pages seduced him. He gathered them up and hid them in his overcoat. Then he exited quickly. Father Oscar saved my life. And he saved the book as well. When the hounds returned—others now, and better educated— the pages were no longer there. The father hid them bravely, risking his own life, much like someone carrying a time bomb. Years later he sent me the originals. Earlier he'd told me he had burned them. From then on, my mother hid those pages covered with corrections and illegible notes, like buildings in construction adorned with cobwebs of scaffolding.

After the border, I roamed the city like a stray dog. A prisoner of permanent frustration, I had decided to escape. My problem was the book in the hands of my aged mother. I wanted to take it, but she adamantly refused. She had hidden it. She wouldn't tell anyone where! She was obsessed by the hounds of the regime. In her dreams, she told me, she had seen them arrive, laden down with putrid nights, rum, and daggers. They would kill her son! And she would continue to hide those papers.

THE POLICE KNOCKED ASSERTIVELY at my door. They were looking for a man. They knocked again. My sister was filled with fear. As my mother opened the door, my sister ran to the courtyard with the pages and buried them, as if sowing seeds of fear. False alarm. "We've got the wrong house," they said curtly. From then on, the book remained buried, yellowed from days and hiding places; yellow like those prisoners who never see the sun.

Then a splendid spring arrived—the sky shattered by rains—just what the country's cattle growers had hoped for, their fields burned, just that for which everyone's hunger had prayed. The water, reminiscent of those ancient floods seen by the old-timers, turned my book into the best sort of fertilizer for the courtyard's ferns. It had been forgotten by everyone. I too had forgotten it, just as certain parents forget their children. Then one day I asked about my book. My sister grew pale. She couldn't remember where she had buried it in her effort to save me! She almost dissolved in tears. We raked through the garden. It didn't appear. At that moment, I felt as if I had lost a child! Finally, it turned up: nothing but a compost heap. Once again, I wanted to weep: torn pages, almost illegible, bits and pieces eaten by insects, shreds turned to dung. My child had shown up at last, deformed, monstrous . . . but mine.

I took its dead body in my hands. With a father's care, I have tried to give it new life. This is the story of that history.

—FREDDY PRESTOL CASTILLO

YOU CAN CROSS THE MASSACRE ON FOOT

1

The teacher had pronounced an unfamiliar word: "*Dajabón...*" It was the name of a village far from where I lived. This was in the class called "Geography of the Nation," and referred to a place on the border between the Dominican Republic and the Republic of Haiti, both situated on the island of Hispaniola or Santo Domingo, one of the Caribbean's Greater Antilles.

The teacher spoke monotonously. He didn't know his country. He was from an illustrious family in the capital and had never been to "those villages." The inhabitants of the capital spoke contemptuously of "those villages" in their own land. Limited to their small colonial city, rife with rancid prestige, they were proud of the fundamentally antinational urban landscape that separated them from the other provinces, villages, and territories. In his tastes, the teacher was a foreigner. In short, an important man of the capital who read the *Times* and exotic magazines about sports, art, and fashion. "This is civilization!" he would say, as he thumbed through those foreign magazines. But *those villages*... "Those villages must be unbearable..."

And a disagreeable expression would come to his thin lips, all of him so like a confessor figure, a frustrated priest. "Those villages, out there . . ." (he was referring to faraway villages with their gray, centuries-old images, beached like broken-down boats upon their landscapes of hills or plains; like old trees that never move, always in a place of honor). *Those villages*, their histories heroic and yellow with age.

The teacher wasn't interested in anything about those villages.

"Dajabón . . . !" The strange name intrigued me, and I wondered what that faraway bit of our territory across from Haiti was like.

WE STUDENTS, children of the rich, lived behind thick and useless white walls; that flat architecture Spain left its poor colony, with neither palaces nor ostentation, no mines or loadbearing Indians. A miserably poor colony that ended up living off the famous handout sent by Mexico. They say our grandparents spent their days looking out to sea, waiting for the galleons that would arrive with wages and aid for the miserable colony. Despite all that, after centuries we became an ostensibly free country, and I and my provincial compatriots, sons of landowners and wealthy merchants, were far removed from it all: from the nation, its dramas; far removed, in short, from Dominican life. Our only interests were Sunday soccer, baseball, tennis. And, above all, we received our instruction from a sonorous authority: the schoolmaster's whistle calling us to order. San Roman School. A tranquil high-society life, like that of the sugar barons on our eastern haciendas.

My father had vast sugarcane fields. I didn't know their landscape, nor the barracks where the black field hands lived, nor the harshness of their sun. I knew nothing of what was inside those sad low shacks.

In my town, I had seen the broad port, profuse with foreign ships that carried sugar to distant lands. I saw the dirty laborers, men who sang sad melodies in the port at dusk, when modern electric lighting illuminated the young and restless city. They seemed like another class of men to me. Their hardness made them repulsive. Still, I watched as they loaded the ships with sugar. Like a child looking through a book with grotesque drawings of strong and dangerous animals.

Back then, sugar was earning astronomical prices on the international market. In the fields, the stalks of cane rose proud, higher than the men who cultivated them. Automobiles and laughter also existed in my town. People chewed gum, spoke English, played tennis, and then frequented the movie houses or exclusive clubs where parties were held. I remember the waltzes at those parties, and the gentlemen's ostentatious manners: the rich merchants of my town. Sometimes, in the middle of a party, the sound of winches and hoarse foghorns of ships could be heard coming from the nearby port. At other times, one could hear the trains that carried sugar to that port. The trains belonging to North American companies ran right through the city, as if it was just another North American hacienda. The street bore a pedestrian name: Locomotive Avenue.

NOW, IN OUR SCHOOL'S refined atmosphere, our consciences were being shaped by a sophisticated teacher, full of vacuous courtesy and lacking any nationalist sense. Look at him there: all measured and refined, like in the stores. His luxurious Sun King's mane, his well-trimmed moustache, always wearing an out-of-style black suit, like a prior's wimple, his surname sonorously colonial. Princely salesman in a gray shell. He spoke slowly and ceremoniously. We thought he must be afraid of everyone, dead and alive. Afraid of governments most of all.

That morning in National Geography class—always a nightmare for him—he spoke about the Dominican Republic's border and said, "Yes, my children, yes . . . ! The border is here . . . [and he pointed with his thick finger]. Here there is a river named El Masacre . . . right across from Haiti." (I watched his thick fingers and carefully cared-for hands that had never swung an ax or handled a horse's bridle.)

BUT THE WEALTH OF the Antilles isn't something mastered here. It is managed on foreign stock exchanges. On these Caribbean islands, where the economy is based on sugar planted and harvested by black labor, there are some astonishing surprises. There, not here, the prices of our products are determined, which means that there, not here, the price of our labor is calculated. Wall Street's market! Pricing court supreme! Roulette wheel that makes a man rich or condemns him to misery.

Our people, who love the sun, approve. A winning ticket and up we go! A losing ticket and we're done for!

And we, the happy inhabitants of Macorís del Mar, had lost at sugarcane poker!

The brilliant and sunny landscape of my town turned gray and nostalgic. Farewell to the exotic sailors, blonde and drunk, who over-flowed the port and its dives. Farewell to the smoke from giant factories. Only memories remained, and isolation.

The jovial city had been transformed. Daggers of hunger pierced the heart of my town, which had seemed like a big gangly and sporting young man, like the Yankee student with his history of machinery, ships, sugar, and blacks as frenetic as the cranes in the port. It's true. We'd lost at sugarcane poker.

Now, after the pause imposed by my father's death, and besieged by economic penury, I went to the old capital to enter the university and pursued my study of the law.

When he died, there were only a few coins left with which to cover the final obligation, that of his burial. We paid for it without asking for help from friends.

How did it happen? Our family wealth, in money, sugarcane fields, and haciendas, had evaporated. My father had decided to pay even his most insignificant debt, to give everything to his creditors, even our ancestral home, the wealthy mansion where we were born. All that was left of our yesterday was my father's unanimous fame in the mouths of bankers, usurers, merchants, and above all the poor. Everyone said he had been "the town's most honorable man."

I returned home to a loneliness, a sad almost macabre tranquility, circumscribed by my mother's expressions and prayers. And then the landscape of the town itself: flat, gray, miserable.

MY REFUGE IS THE tavern favored by the workers of Santa Barbara, in the rundown hotel belonging to Teodora Jáquez, a black woman who is half matchmaker, half holy woman and always mindful of the pain of others. A poor tavern frequented by a few provincial students but mainly workers, men from the port and the factories, who show up tired, with the urge to shout and accuse, but who remain silent.

In Santo Domingo, expressing one's thoughts is prohibited. We are allowed to speak only if we are going to praise the President. At the bar, my country's basest words: the lewd story, the high-pitched libidinous songs of the Caribbean, and the broad white smiles of blacks and mulattos, strong as bulls. Most, landless peasants or owners of some small parcel in litigation, talked about their rights and looked for unknown grandfathers, swallowed by years, from whom they might inherit. None of them work the land. They are all selling it. And, a last resort, the port. These are my café companions: ex-peasants. Now they are stevedores, watchmen, idiots of every vice, especially alcohol, which consumes everything they earn. The tavern is picturesque: the latest song, the ghostly prostitute retired and reduced to begging now, the waiter who greets us with *hey* or with *what's up* because he does not understand the meaning of respect or courtesy. And in the corner, the students' pale faces.

We students talked and dreamed. Of what? Our future, the nation's problems, the country's social situation. We had to do this discreetly, for fear of being denounced, which commonly meant death. Illusions, hopes . . . !

I COULDN'T PAY THE taxes that would have enabled me to obtain my degree. Everyone else had been able to do so. I saw even the most ignorant of my classmates become the head of some important law firm. Despite my brilliant academic grades, I walked the streets, looking for someone who might take pity and give me the few pesos I needed to get my degree and pass the bar. There was no one. I thought then—and still think—this is a land without gentlemen.

I went out into the plaza. There was a political debate going on. Everyone talked politics. Everyone unanimously praised the President. I thought one of those gentlemen might be able to help me. I remembered that my friend, a well-known poet, had introduced me to one of those important individuals. The generous man listened to me with a kindness uncommon among the emissaries of power in this country. He gave me hope. I should wait until he was able to arrange for my entrance into the judicial service. Then I would be able to take a seat on the tribunal of Santo Domingo or one of the provinces, in Macorís del Mar, for example. It might also happen that the powers that be, who didn't know me, could arrange for me to go to some remote village. . . . Who was I, after all . . . ? A young and unknown lawyer!

The truth is, politics is a thing of chance, a deck of cards. And the cards didn't favor me. The order came: go to Dajabón, the remote village across from Haiti, which that effeminate teacher had described in my childhood as some nondescript place.

SO HERE YOU HAVE ME, in a battered old car heading toward Dajabón. An old model—naturally—because no one would send a new car to such a desert habitat. Only remains of cars and remains of men travel to such places. Failed bureaucrats, lesser types, second-class teachers, tired old lawyers, in short, the system's leftovers. That's where I'm going. What will become of me . . . ?

AFTER SANTIAGO, A SUNNY HIGHWAY. Sad towns, and dry. Here, I thought, one would have to investigate life by means of secondhand equations. Skinny children, like ghosts. Algebraic goats. Low brown shacks made from cane. Sun, sun, sun! Everything beaten down by the sun. Turns in the asphalt now. Some crosses in a local shrine. And at last! The old and beloved sea.

When I asked the driver the name of the town, he said: "Monte Cristy."*

A sleepy town by the sea.

This had been the tragic site of our battles for emancipation and civil wars. I notice its formal yet attractive landscape, its friendly people who still know how to smile, and I think about their history, from the sixteenth-century exoduses ordered by Don Antonio de Osorio to frustrated commerce with the "heretics" who violated the prohibitions of the judgments of Santo Domingo and the mandates of the king. It was just about there that I felt like nodding off, as the car continued on its way. (My destiny was farther on, still deeper into the countryside.)

More isolation. The distance begins to impose itself upon my spirit. I sense the border, that land that none of the so-called wise men of my country know, only my country's soldiers—the "guards"—and barefoot laborers with neither shoes nor conscience.

DAJABÓN AT LAST!

A village of cane toasted by the island's strongest sun. Straw-colored town with an indigenous imprint, its three empty and drowsy streets ending at the banks of El Masacre, where the people wash their clay-covered feet.

Is no one here . . . ? Only a few souls. Almost all have fled. Here people have been emigrating since colonial times. I see frightened blacks, mute mouths.

A park, with robust laurel trees, like the hungry strapping sons of the town peddler. And . . . silence.

What happens in Dajabón . . . ?

---

* Spelling of the era.

"The Cutting"* was going on then. The Cutting...! What did that even mean...? No one had bothered to explain it to me. Not even the innkeeper herself. Later I would learn everything.

Today the old mail car brought an extra package. It was me! I was destined for the village Court of Law.

---

* I have translated *el Corte* as the Cutting. This was the massacre of October 1937, carried out against Haitians living in the Dominican Republic's northwestern frontier and in certain parts of the contiguous Cibao region by Dominican Army troops on the direct orders of dictator Rafael Trujillo. It is also sometimes referred to as the Parsley Massacre.

2

I didn't know about the depressive power my country's savannah had upon one's spirit. I have traveled the length and breadth of it, the last boundary of the old Marién holding. I have roamed like a dead man through the final days of my judgeship. I traveled those brown-gray scrublands where the cow abandoned by its owner grazes day after day on hard bristly grass, tenacious beneath the sun, the *maicoté*. It left me with a bitter and mystical taste of sorrow. I felt numbed and sad.

Sad cows—why did the cows seem so sad?—*maicoté* and sun. There are no more Haitian laborers now. Ever since Captain Windbag started "the Cutting," the Haitians have disappeared. The Cutting! What trembling and terror I saw on more than one thick mulatto lip, in more than one combination of ambiguous sounds made in an effort to speak good Spanish, to demonstrate that the person speaking was Dominican!

"The Cutting . . ." You might as well say the Exodus. What afternoons of dust and sun! And long nights. (Night stretched out as if to aid and abet the crime. Awake in my bed, I longed for dawn. But dawn didn't come. Night was endless, overwhelming me.)

The Captain drank and drank and drank. And the savannah was huge, immense. All the dead fit on the savannah.

"Sargeeeennt . . . ! Sargent Pío . . ."

"Here, my Captain!"

The Captain staggered as he spoke; he was drunk. He made an effort in his drunkenness, and in the dark realm of his mind a red light appeared, like a bloody sun. Trying hard, he answered the greeting and told the Sargent:

"I just receive a serio order. The government say cut the throat of every *mañese* we find. They no respect order, what the hell. We burn 'em live. Eh . . . ! Sargento . . . ! It's Captain Windbag talking! A drink! Anyone you find, bring 'em in! Understand! We gonna burn 'em live . . . !"

Captain Windbag couldn't bear the weight of the tragedy he'd been given. He was charged with painting that whole countryside red, prairie and hills. In assuming his role as Attila, he took to the bottle. Killing thousands! Old people, children, women . . . Why? He didn't know. It was an "order."

At one point, he remembered that his grandfather was born in Haiti . . . ! And he downed almost half a bottle of rum. His lips still trembled, and he gazed out over the savannah like an idiot.

ANTA AND OLD SURIEL are one and the same. But Anta is more poetic. Anta on the banks of El Masacre, where she washes and sings. Breasts as hard as the almonds of the arroyo. Hips like one of the mules at the agricultural farm. Orchestra of sweets, supple ass, and a deep voice heard singing on the banks of the river.

Captain Pirulí say
he'll be comin' tonight. . . .
Leave the door open
and his shirt wash' . . .

This is the Dominican side of the river. El Masacre,* a small river that separates two countries.

Marcelle at that small river, El Masacre. Marcelle washes and looks suspiciously across to the other side. Marcelle, the Haitian woman. It seems she's still afraid.

Suunsuá . . . Suunsuá, papá . . .

Suunsuá . . .

Marcelle, the Haitian. Escaped from the Cutting. She's washing in El Masacre, that small international river. Beside Marcelle is the mangy dog, Pití. A Haitian dog, a runner, a fugitive, light as the dry *chachá* leaf.

Since her escape, Marcelle hasn't heard from her parents. The Sargent, from the fort, said her father was a cattle thief. Marcelle the Haitian says nothing.

Anta Suriel, the black queen, also knows nothing of her Haitian boyfriend, Daniel the tinsmith. In Dajabón he was also a shoemaker. Where is Daniel? Buried on the savannah. Anta doesn't know where. If she knew, she would have gone to stick a cross in the savannah's brown earth. Daniel was good. Legbá! Haiti's Papá Legbá will protect him.

Clear river; sometimes ochre, sometimes green. And sometimes the color of wine. A river with secrets. El Masacre.

DANIEL'S DRAMA HAD BEEN that of the entire black community living on the prairies and in the mountains. What was that community like? A tribe of nomadic shepherds and farmers that had finally settled on the far-off and forgotten land along the Dominican Republic's border, just across from Haiti. Those blacks had arrived at the very limits of the rustic holdings of the Dominican ranchers who settled Dajabón and its surrounding villages, eventually assuming the idle lives of landowners who lived off the work of Haitian laborers.

* El Masacre, literally "the massacre," is the name of the river, as differentiated from the massacre referring to the wanton killing of thousands in October 1937.

For example, all the horses belonging to García, a man rich in lands that had never been cultivated, had been raised by the Haitian mule driver Toussant. The same was true of Don Chepe's cow farm. His tan and spotted cows had been pampered and sweet-talked by Tamí Pié. Meanwhile, Don Chepe, the owner, a dark-skinned creole who came from a long line of Spanish and Haitian ancestors, took his siestas at his large house beneath the shade of the old trees growing there. Only Tamí ventured out into the fields, and the rebellious mules obeyed him alone. Other laborers brought the crops to Don Chepe's house. Seen from Don Chepe's mansion, life was monotonous and without incident, its fields green when it rained and doggedly gray-brown in the summer. Don Chepe wasn't interested in the "Dominican Republic." He was content with his own land, his cows and crops, all worked by Haitian blacks. His only concern, in fact, was a place on the town's "Honorable Council."

The Haitians ate fruit off the trees and threw their seeds on the ground. New trees were born. Many trees. And in the Haitian barracks more Haitians were born, many Haitians. The land produced Haitians and trees.

In time, the Haitian became "the man," as the popular expression went. And he was satisfied in this rustic Arcadia where they sometimes speak a Spanish the laborers barely understand. The songs come from Haiti. The skin has a copper color that results from the mix of our blacks and Haitians. All the young black daughters of the grandest of the town's society matrons had married Haitians. And these held all the jobs: hotel manager, shoemaker, farmer, and laborer. In the hills, there was also a community in which all the landowners were Haitian.

THE CAPTAIN WAS STILL drunk that morning, and the sergeants and their men proceeded to carry out his orders. Among them, besides Sargent Pío, was another they called the Cruel One. His nickname said it all. He possessed the shrewdness of a drunken panther unable to distinguish between what was good and what was criminal.

He was a minor figure when compared with Sargent Pío, who gazed upon the sundrenched land with his sick eyes. Sargent Tarragona: he had the artistry of a cat combined with a tiger's speed. Still, he is worried: he's been given the order to "burn everything." Meaning he must kill, demolish, and finally burn to the ground all the houses and their inhabitants.

THE SAVANNAH IS HUGE. The ID card, a document required by Santo Domingo law, would be the pretext. The soldiers would round people up, looking for anyone who lacked that document, and so drive great masses of Haitians from distant fields. Away from the villages they would more easily be able to carry out their homicidal party. The Haitians came quietly, in long lines. Old men, like the beggar Tamí, young people and girls with hardened skin and underarm stench. Peasant clothes of every color. All the while, the soldiers kept drinking their rum.

"Boys . . . come on . . . come on! We have a job to do," the Sargent said, while saluting his men almost without looking up. Everyone was drinking.

The blacks went obediently to slaughter. They knew that clemency was impossible.

Death's tragedy muffled screams of horror. Terror, death rattles. And silence. And then the screams of others whose turn had come. One shouted: "Don't kill on me . . . Me Dominiquén . . . !"

"Don't kill . . . here, take" (he offered money).

One of the drunken soldiers, the devil himself, shouted: "Hands up . . . don' waste my time . . . ! Damned *mañé*!"

"Ah, dear God . . ." and he fell.

The knives kept on swinging, across a vast territory. Those wielding them were farm laborers themselves who, before becoming soldiers, had learned to clear fields in the villages. The full range of their art rose now, tragic and implacable.

One shouted: "Don' kill, Pié . . . Don't kill me . . . !"

"Shut up, yo' black devil . . . !"

And the deaf music of daggers continued beneath the sun, while frightened bees fled their apiaries.

Ferocious ten o'clock sun, wounding sun of the northwest, while a whole people succumbs like stalks in an immense cornfield.

"Boys! Onward . . . ! Let's finish off these black parasites who have taken the land from Dominicans! Onward!"

The Sargent shouted. In his drunken stupor, at the moment of sacrificing Haitian blacks, something surged inexplicably from his subconscious: "These blacks are good . . . but they are thieves! They must die!"

This was the red harvest. Ordered by the Captain. What the Captain's boss ordered and the boss of them all . . . the Dominican Republic's boss.

"Damn!" said a sergeant from Mao—wild-eyed, rude-mannered, hair every which way, a "colored man": "Damnnn . . . ! I gonna remember my time, when the General attack the Santiago Fort . . . fighting with my teeth . . . ! Pity these damn '*mañé*' don' fight . . . ! But what I gonna do with this little parrot. . . . They gonna have to make me general . . . !"

"Little parrot" was what he called his long knife. The Sargent came out onto the patio. On this border, night seems like another world. A temperate night. Dogs howling in the distance. At times, snatches of merengue, even farther in the distance. Behind the military quarters, an owl makes a scandal. Sargent Elonginio talks to himself. Elonginio: a killer. But now, in the silence, he remembers his young children, naked, their bellies full of parasites, barefoot, who don't go to school, back in a shack in the capital. Sargent Elonginio, then, waxes tender.

Night falls slowly. On a sad and desolate land. For days now, the birds don't sing; it seems they have abandoned this place.

Suddenly the silence is broken. From the depths of the patio a melody can be heard. A sergeant they call Devil Woman sings in his hoarse drunken voice, accompanied by an old accordion:

Ay, Siña Juanica
for God sake, Siña Juanica . . .
my child is dyin'
I ain' got no medicine . . .

The night wears on, even more temperate. When the drunken man stops singing, all that can be heard are the eternal crickets and the changes of command:

"Atenshun!"

"Halt!"

"Atenshun!"

"Halt!"

3

The Captain has new executioners. One of them is Manuel Robert. Young, energetic, built like an athlete, like a *jaiquí*, hardwood tree of the Northwest Frontier.

The troop surprised him returning from the *tumba*. He would open a plot in brown fields, thick with brambles and brush, on lands belonging to old Juanico Rivas. How long he'd suffered, how many agonies he'd endured, to be able to clear that plot . . . ! Naked and alone, he dug those graves, with almost nothing to eat. Now and then he smoked bad tobacco. He left his house on foot before dawn and went with his ax and his pipe to that lonely place. But they were good lands, those of old man Juanico. Black earth like that of Moca, with small lakes. That's why he promised half a harvest to the proprietor and usurer.

The owner, Juanico Rivas, was old now but typically miserly. Those from around there said he owned more cows than he had hairs on his body, and that he'd inherited them from his father, General Rivas, a revolutionary from the region. He kept his ounces of gold in pillowcases and spent his days astride an old mule, visiting farms and drinking coffee, in a picturesque attitude somewhere between that of potentate and beggar. Like all those of his class along the border, he didn't work the land. He kept himself going with repeated sips of coffee and plates of yucca grown by others on his estate.

Times had changed for Juanico. The cattle had disappeared. On the one hand, because of the wars, the "revolutions" that killed livestock and men. Another reason for the cattle's demise was Haitian thievery. Juanico professed poverty, but it was the typical peasant claim. He owned the best lands from La Carbonera, Joussard, Doña María, and Santiago de la Cruz to Partido y Vaca Gorda, where his great estates ended. He had never planted a blade of grass.

Now he made his rounds, a great Leontine watch on a gold chain in his pocket, his pipe, a worn big-brimmed hat, and a crosswise captain's sable.

"I need talk to my General . . . that *mañé* (the Haitians) has done me in . . . ! I don't have one sheep, one bull left standing . . . and for a while now I can't walk on the savannah . . . 'cause this whole place was a solid mass of cattle. . . . Ah! those *mañé* devils . . . ! Night before last they was here, and not one stalk of yucca left for my poor blacks, or for me. . . . Them Haitian work for the Devil. . . . They walk with night as if it day . . . !"

The old man was ignorant of what was happening in Juan Calvo and Doña María.

That morning he waited in vain for Manuel Robert. The soldiers had taken him prisoner. Then they came for the old man.

"How can I help you . . . ?"

"Go on, walk!" commanded an alcoholic voice. "And don't ask questions . . . is an order! And pick yourself up . . . show us you still a man!"

A long white caliche road, where Juanico Rivas walks with guards on either side. Where is he going . . . ? He doesn't know. Will he too be going to kill Haitians?

4

Morning surprised the Captain and his acolytes with their eyes open. Cowardly is the guard who doesn't sleep, with his mix of thick words and alcohol. The Captain wanted his eyes to be lenses through which he might disrobe the night's mysteries, in wait along the route that moves off to the left of El Masacre on its way to the Haitian village of Juana Méndez. Will they come? Will the Haitians come to take revenge on their neighbors . . . ?

With uncertainty, another drink. Fear hid itself in the tavern beneath a Dante-like display of shiny weapons and servile smiles.

At that moment, our Captain is like a god, posing in a shithole of a shack by El Masacre. Windbag has come up in the world. The anonymous boy who once roamed threadbare beneath the oaks in the capital's plazas is now a man. What's more: he is Caligula, who, bloody with crime, has become part of our history, here, on the far-off prairie and in the green mountains of the borderland.

That's why hours have passed in the greasy spoon, between the laughter of café companions and praise for the Captain. Mean-

while, the village slept. Among those café companions were Manuel
Mejía and Francisco Espartero, obliged to remain at the Captain's
side. It's tyranny! Our country has an iron noose around its neck
and the executioner's ax is poised above every head! Who is the
executioner . . . ? Anyone! This one or that. First, the snitch. Then any
strong kid from the countryside who abandoned the land in search
of fortune and now has the new butcher's mission: that of killing his
brother, his father, his friend. And that's Windbag: a butcher.

When the Captain leaves, it's the end of the nightmare for Lauterio,
for Francisco, and for Rafael Mejía. He's leaving! He's drunk! He drank
all night, until the sun came up. And they watch him go. These good
men of the village look at one another. They are landowners who have
lived all their lives off the slave labor of Haitians, and now they are left
with immense estates without anyone to work them! They look at one
another in silence. As if they want to say: "Good riddance, Captain!"

But they don't speak, as they walk slowly home where their wives
and children have waited for them filled with fear through the night.

When he got to the corner, Rafael Mejía, who was obese and had
never spent much time at the tavern, was desperate to buy a bottle.
He's drunk now, but in his fear of the government he remains concerned for his personal safety. As he stumbles at the corner, he thinks
he sees a spy following him. Don Rafael, somewhere between drunk
and sober, looks up. His eyes betray him. Then, potbellied and awkward, he shouts: "Long live Trujillo!"

(And he repeats it three times, as if conjuring a hellish beast.)

The Captain's car—the only one in the village—moves through
the dirt streets compelled by a false urgency.

A few people look through the cracks between the palm boards
from which almost all the houses are constructed. Some are still
afraid, because Haitians are hidden in those houses. Will prisoners or
reservists come to search where they live . . . ?

Daggers and clubs have prevented the Haitians from escaping to
their own country, Haiti. The order was: Kill them. The Haitians
mustn't be allowed to return to their country. They must remain on
the savannah, like the lush mango trees they planted. The only hope is

night, which might serve as cover for one or another lucky one who'd hidden long hours inside the old oven of a house where he'd been born, or in some woman's bedroom that hadn't been searched.

Black Moraime Luis had grown up with the town's innkeeper. That afternoon, at the news of the beheadings, she trembled in fright. What should she do? Try to leave . . . ? Escape, run toward Haiti . . . ? But . . . how? The soldiers were vigilant, on patrol across from the fort, on the road leading out of town toward Juana Méndez, the village closest to the border. . . . Where should she go . . . ? She's in the same fix as Yusén, the shoemaker. He is from Haiti but doesn't have anyone there.

Moraime Luis doesn't know her relatives in Haiti either. She is the daughter of a Haitian washwoman they made leave the inn's patio this very afternoon. Her body, tossed in the river, was carried by the current all the way to widow Tabale's estate. What should she do . . . ?

Flee! Her only recourse.

The innkeeper told her: "Be careful, Moraime! If they see you, they will kill you! Hide under my bed! Hurry!"

The black girl ran to hide beneath the bed of the innkeeper, a member of Dajabón society's elite. That's what saved her.

A few minutes later the patrol appeared, looking for the black girl. They had come through the patio's open gate.

"Mistress Francina . . . ! We come looking for her . . . ! That black girl . . . ! On Captain's order. . . . Hand her over now, 'cause we gotta go to the savannah . . . in the Captain's . . . service. . . ."

The most terrifying of the prisoners was speaking: the Cat, condemned to thirty years for murder and robbery. Now he was free. An executioner.

Mistress Francina lied admirably. She said the black girl had run and they'd probably killed her crossing El Masacre.

The Cat believed her and was about to leave. He was thirsty and made for the great water tank near which poor Moraime was hiding. He hesitated for a moment, sniffing around like a trapped animal that senses it has come upon its prey. He stopped speaking and seemed undecided, looking at the woman. He looked at her again. At last, he decided to leave. As he did, he uttered these words: "I wanted to find that girl, make her pay . . . ! I always wanting her, but she always refuse, call me mangy dog . . . ! And that woman care for her like her own child . . . seem like she wanna marry her to some white so she can't belong to the Cat. . . ."

The Cat went out onto the savannah. And the woman packed up Moraime's things so she could escape. Moraime cried. Where could she go . . . ?

She must move carefully. She would make her way through the streets, through the courtyards of the houses. When she got to the town square, she would have to hide behind the benches. When she came to the church, she would be able to take refuge inside if someone passed.

When she got there, she thought: This is my church!

They had baptized her there, in Spanish. Yes, she was Dominican! Why did she have to leave . . . ?

And she was tempted to shout as loud as she could: *No! No! I am Dominican! This is my country . . . ! That's not my country . . . !*

She heard the soldiers going by and restrained herself in time.

Now she has reached the last street, rounding the fort. She carries the bag her mistress prepared and a few coins she's given her.

"Run . . . ! Run . . . !" she'd told her, between the sobs her soul had tried to hide.

"*Bon dieu* . . . I must leave Francén. . . . She is my mother. . . . She raised me . . . !"

She goes on. She's about to come to the banks of El Masacre. She will cross the river near the corral belonging to her friends, the Rocas. (There the cows are as frightened as the people. Can the animals sense this tragedy?)

When she'd almost crossed the river, almost made it to freedom, a mangy dog, one of those that roam along its shores, denounced her with its hungry barking. The troop, with its orders, drunk on rum and blood, does not forgive.

The black girl's terrified screams reached the home of the woman who had tried to save her, loud and clear. Powerful screams, lamentations in two languages, like El Masacre itself that sang to the two peoples living along its banks.

"*Pardón . . . ! Pardón . . . ! Dieu . . . ! Dieu . . . !* Don't kill me. . . . Don't kill me. . . . Take my money . . . ! Take my money . . . ! Don't kill me . . . !"

And she offered the coins. In vain.

Moraime Luis lost her virginity on the sands of the river's shore. Looking for freedom. She also lost her life. Meanwhile, the soldiers continued to swill their rum. And night fell, silent as a fine rain. Now and then, a burst of gunfire. No use, at that point, to ask about a single black girl. The river helps hide the crime. It carries her body away. Where? Anywhere, until it is devoured by mountain swine and vagabond dogs.

5

In that dump of a town, the news of Moraime Luis's death spread. She was the black girl who worked at the inn that belonged to fine Mistress Francina. The small hotel suffered the effects of the incident: they had murdered every black girl raised by its owner, a stalwart of the community. An early widow, skilled in working with horses and other ranch jobs, her foreign husband, dead before his time, had left her longing for love. Mistress Francina had no children.

Here is a brief description of that interesting woman: her long hair was black; her thirst for love undying. She is a picture of calculation and presumed modesty. She possesses a calm smile, like gentle rain. Determined, and into everything. Until she learned everything she needed to know. She says that love passed her by some time ago, and so her beautiful eyelashes shade her brilliant eyes like a bright window suddenly closed in the night. Nothing stopped her from covering herself with Christian cloth and attending the first mass of the day.

Mistress Francina wore the clothes of dignity in that village; she was a respectable woman. In her youth, she had been the wife of a

Dane by the name of Mr. Broberg. That foreigner, whose history was as incomplete as a book with missing pages, had a sailor's biography that had taken him to Monte Cristy in search of hardwood. That's where he eventually dropped anchor and where, instead of a ship's pilot and tuna diver, he became a merchant, an inland boss.

Broberg later does well. In this country "land is cheap and men barely want to work it." Broberg travels. He reaches the town of Dajabón and puts down roots: he liked the land and was sure that in these Antilles, despite what the politicians said and what he read in the papers, it was still easy for men to exploit other men. Above all, there are some beings who could hardly be called men: the Haitian blacks, cheap labor.

Mr. Broberg stayed. At home, he kept cellars filled with good French wines imported from the Haitian city, Cap Haitiene. At the same time, his crops did well and his cattle filled whole fields. That is, until the frequent revolutions came along. Young and wealthy, Mr. Broberg married Mistress Francina, a beautiful Indian of the village. Mr. Broberg had traded the blue, almond-shaped eyes of Helssen, his Danish lady friend, for the dark ones of his warm creole. A good trade . . . ? It seemed so. Mistress Francina managed the fields, the laborers, the money, and, it goes without saying, Mr. Broberg himself.

But Mr. Broberg died young. He left his creole halfway through her initiation into love's mysteries. And all this happened in the torrid atmosphere of Dajabón, where this island's hottest sun requires endless siestas beneath its great laurel trees. Later, Mistress Francina must have suffered terrible nights of loneliness. (Mistress Francina is someone who loves intensely, hates intensely, and has an admirable ability to hide her insatiable female need.) When people speak about her lovers, they downplay her emotions and do not mention that she hides them in the same way as she dyes the gray in her hair. Mistress Francina has one desire, to remain young forever. Why? Didn't Mr. Broberg die a long time ago?

Mistress Francina has decided that the best business through which she would be able to control the lives of others is the inn. People talk about everything there. Her inn is the most prestigious in town. It is a semi-feudal business, organized and sustained by a bevy of young slaves: her stepdaughters, the daughters of Haitian laborers, brought to be raised at Mistress Francina's house. From time to time, fate will deposit some diplomat at the inn, on his way to or from Haiti, and he must spend the night in Dajabón.

Also living on the premises are the young magistrates brought by the government as soon as that far-off territory became a province, full of glory in the nation's history. All this makes for sociability, Mistress Francina's greatest delight. It can also become an occasion on which a confession of love responds to a night of loneliness. A young magistrate, coming back half-drunk at night, forgot which room was his and accidentally entered another. At that moment, he might be met by a declaration of love. An unexpected offer: the young magistrate is confused. Poor Mr. Broberg! Customarily, he attended to his business. "Such a nice man . . . ," but this chance encounter is delicious. An interesting landlady from a distant land, a woman of energetic semblance, fully in charge, filled with the gossip of politics and love. Yes, why not, love . . . ? The next morning, she rises late. It doesn't matter: the black girls take care of everything. The most faithful of them all being Moraime Luis, killed by the prisoners when she tried to cross the river to Haiti.

When this landlady awakens with her noble face—pale mahogany—that was beautiful once and remains so with the help of makeup, she is the picture of honesty. She goes to church then. End of story.

She attends to the recently arrived with a French courtesan's smile. She radiates the vibrant blood of a woman of the northeast, forged in the style created by Mr. Broberg. He left her a lot of cattle, a lot of blacks, and a large ranch. Mistress Francina is a great lady. With her servants she rarely speaks Spanish, almost always Creole. She turns her mischievous face to a guest and asks him if he is married or single: "Here . . . you will suffer a lot, because this is a backwater town . . . but we will treat you as if you are in your own home. . . . God knows, you may miss me when you leave . . . !"

And she wore an intensely feminine expression as she ordered the maids—in Patois*—to take the newcomer's bags: a young judge of twenty-eight, and unmarried!

IMPORTANT PEOPLE VISIT THE house at night. One of them is Don Sebusto.† President of the local government, large landowner, a conservative man whose hacienda has been left without laborers. Who will take care of all those cattle . . . ? Don Sebusto introduces the subject into the conversation: "We've never seen the likes of this, Francina! How are we going to live . . . ? Don't they like the Haitians . . . ? What have those good blacks ever done to them . . . ? As you see me now, I'm about ready to leave, to sell everything and go to the capital, where my parents are. . . . But who can I sell to?"

Then he looks around, wary about having criticized the government for throwing out the Haitians.

He continues: "Daughter, we can't live like this. . . . Dajabón is finished . . . and the government is levying taxes on top of taxes. . . . At my house, it's been years since we've had any wine from Broberg's cellar! We can barely dress decently. And I, who only wore Haitian silk. . . . It's the same with the commercial patents. . . . Inspectors coming around all the time to check. . . . We weren't accustomed to this. . . . We enjoyed free trade with Haiti. . . . Customs were a formality. Well, not a formality, but not like now. We even brought fish from Haiti. And what wines! Broberg, poor thing, was always drunk on good wine. . . . He'd be desperate now! And remember: our blacks weren't plagued by Health Services, there were no regulations like we have now, and we lived so well . . . ! Now there are health certificates and a thousand other things. . . . What are we going to do . . . ?"

---

* The local Haitian language was called Patois at the time of the history this book tells. Now that it is acknowledged as a language, it is called Creole or Kreyol. I used "Patois" throughout.

† In Spanish, Don and Doña are prefixes of respect, much like Sir and Mistress or Madam in English. I have chosen to leave Don in Spanish throughout.

This is every night's conversation: longing for the good old days, when the government hardly showed its face in these far-off lands. Dialogues beneath the stars, because there's no electricity in Dajabón. Everyone uses kerosene lanterns, which isn't a problem for these friends, nothing compared to former times, when there was no danger of revolutions that scattered a great number of cattle and caused as much of a problem for Dajabón's owner class as the exodus or massacre of their Haitian workers.

Don Lauterio enters the conversation. He is the buyer of coffee from Restauración. Once again, he repeats his thesis: "We don't need schools, we need free trade with Haiti." He echoes the history of his grandfather: "He didn't know how to write the letter *O* . . . and he left a hacienda with more cows than he could count. . . ." And he falls silent. From what is said, you understand that for these good people it would have been better to remain a territory, no need to become a province, that new designation that only brought bureaucracy—second-class employees, a few old judges, some young functionaries, plus taxes and more state control.

Blacks who were paid so little they were almost slaves, free trade that allowed the contraband of good wines and cloth, and coffee from Restauración, a highland region where the berries grow splendidly, cultivated by Haitians who sell them cheaply after unloading their cargo at the edges of mountain precipices. What's more, the coffee from Restauración can be purchased with your hand on the scale. . . .

Don Lauterio spoke: "Yes, Francina . . . ! I remember the days of Broberg's cellar . . . but taxes have killed commerce now. The vigilance . . . and all these laws. . . . We're finished here . . . !

This was every night's conversation. There were times, however, when Don Sebusto and Don Lauterio repressed their thoughts. They half doubted their hostess, a great friend of all the captains and regional bosses sent by the government. . . . Might she not be capable of betrayal . . . ? But they soon let go of their concern, and in that intimacy Don Sebusto and Don Lauterio reproached themselves. They believed she was to be trusted. She was, after all, the wife of that good Dane, Mr. Broberg, who had adored her. They remembered that among the Dane's delights was that of putting his wife on a horse. She was a good rider and crack shot. And then he suddenly died one day. Could it have been poison . . . ? Some had whispered that. But no, it was a lie. God had called Mr. Broberg home! Enough of these doubts about the good woman! And so the conversation continued the following night.

But on this one, almost no one spoke. Mistress Francina was devastated by the news of Moraime Luis's death. "Damned government." "Poor Moraime!" (That night she spoke French, as if in soliloquy, almost unconscious of Don Lauterio's presence.)

"Dajabón est mort. . . . Mort, Dajabón. . . . Ce son assasins. Assasins . . . ! Cette gouvernement . . . !"

And, finally, in Spanish:

"What will become of Dajabón . . . ? Will everyone die of hunger . . . ? This government . . . !" She looked around as if worried about spies, then continued to speak. "Why do the good blacks have to leave . . . ? They work for almost nothing. . . . Those good workers cleaned a tract of land for ten cents . . . sometimes even just for a basket of sweet potatoes . . ."

That night Don Sebusto hadn't been there; he'd been absent for a while. Mistress Francina had seen him staggering about, as if drunk. This seemed strange to Mistress Francina, who knows that Don Sebusto doesn't drink. He is a gentleman who carefully keeps his ounces of gold, what he earns from selling his cattle, and only spends time at church and the inn. Don Sebusto only accompanied the Captain on his drinking sprees out of fear.

"Goodbye . . . ! Don Sebusto . . . !" Mistress Francina's tone was a question, imperious.

Don Sebusto understood and came around, filled with fear and with firewater, a bit ridiculous.

"Francina . . . ," he said. "Francina . . . ! It's the Devil who's come to punish us . . . ! I'm leaving with my family! This is terrible . . . ! And we must take care to avoid anyone betraying us! They'll mix you up in something, and when you least expect it they'll 'liquidate' you . . . ! Imagine, they killed all my foremen . . . ! What can I do . . . ? I'm going crazy! And having to spend all day and all night drinking with that man! I must leave, if only to grab myself a bourbon, to go begging in the capital or in La Vega."

Don Sebusto reeled off his sorrows. At the tavern, the Captain had called him a thief. And then asked him for a loan. . . . That was the last straw . . . !

"Francina . . . I'm going to have a heart attack. Imagine, they even slit old Jean Pié's throat, and he's eighty years old. . . . And the same with the black girls. We didn't have any milk in the house today. The calves are nursing and making a fool out of me. . . . Worms have infested my cattle, and I can't find help because not even the Dominicans are willing. They've taken black men over to Juan Calvo and killed them. . . . What's happening? Not a laborer to be had! Because even the Dominicans have had to hide. . . . If they don't, they'll recruit them into the reserves and force them to commit crimes."

At hearing Don Sebusto talk like this all over town, Mistress Francina becomes desperate. And Don Sebusto, under the effects of the alcohol, keeps on talking:

"They've ruined my brother Juanico! His beautiful fields . . . the birds will eat his harvest . . . the parrots, because there's no one to pick his corn and the guinea hens are eating it all. . . . He's got a big peanut field too. If no one harvests it, the nuts will come back on the stalk. . . . There are no laborers. . . . Men! What is this! And tell me, Francina, what have those poor blacks ever done . . . ?"

"Don't keep talking like that, Don Sebusto, you'll only make it worse . . . ! Hold your tongue," Mistress Francina begged.

"No, no," responded Don Sebusto. "I'll die . . . ! My cow is so sick it frightens me. . . . And I had three blacks, poor guys, who knew how to cure it. . . . And the three are lying headless there in the corral. . . . Do you remember Alberto . . . ? That colored kid we raised at the house. . . . They beat him to death . . . ! I found him in the brush, eaten by dogs . . . ! And Sabá, the tall one who wove the cane roofs . . . the same. And Barahona, the darky who was so good at breaking horses . . . beaten. . . . This is the Devil, come to finish us off . . . ! And now I must drink . . . ! I'm not used to it: to avoid them talking, to avoid scandal and their saying one is against the government, which is even worse!"

Late night. Don Sebusto has gone, and Mistress Francina has ceased her supplications. The lament of the haciendas dies down. What can he do, he asks himself, as he staggers home. Dajabón sleeps. And the Captain drinks, drinks, drinks . . .

6

The villages are beautiful on moonlit nights. In the cities one almost never sees the moon. Still, it must be lovely in my country's capital as well, beneath the groves of trees, when it shines like a delicate cotton snowflake.

That moon is the city's rare jewel, beneath its branches, along its elegant avenues. And here, in the town of Manuel Bueno . . . it is silence, quiet on the landscape and across the green plain, which is also the red plain now.

The town's burnt houses are shut tight, asleep, and beneath the trees of the buckthorn forest sleep Sargent Pío Tarragona, his soldiers, and his prisoners. They all seem dyed in silver. Is there a serenity in those men? The pipes are lit. One of them utters occasional sonorous words in his firewater voice: the same who stretches his arms because they hurt from the rigors of the crime. The other, as if crazed, speaks vagaries. It's a strange picture. They are the crime's henchmen. Exhausted and hopeless, like the rest of the world's workers.

Apart, alone, the Sargent smokes in the night. A group of dissidents is a bit farther off. They speak.

"Brother Venancio... I'm sorry... tired...! The more black we kill, we have to kill more and more...! This the Devil! Feel like it not gonna end...! My poor children... ain't even eaten when they trap me.... I'm going over to Mariano Cestero when they stop me and give me that dagger. And me thinking it for killing a bull... but it for killing people. And fucking Pío, never satisfy, calling us chicken...! I'm ready to get out...! My wife with child, my kids dying of hunger, 'cause the field she dry... I say! And didn't they say they was gonna divide up the houses of the blacks...? But nothing...!"

The other sounded off the same, beaten down and disgusted.

"You're not telling me nothing... Brother Loreto... I'm tired of this damn government...! Making killers of us, fucking shit! My heart hurting from so much atrocity! I used to be churchman in Dajabón, and I help the priest, name of Fermín Pére, who they tell me hung up his frock and be a general, now he a senator.... He been a priest in Dajabón.... I not used to this atrocity. Gonna be some mess here...! 'Cause for killing we have the prisoners, who use to killing and like killing...! I come to the border 'cause I don't have no land to work... not for killing peoples. My name is Ruperto de la Cruz, from over Villalobo.... Us de la Cruz, we no thieves or assassins...."

Another spoke up:

"I'm no saint or educate like you, 'cause I was force to kill two or three who attack me to kill... but if you gonna get rid of the black, they should give us something...! Make us captain...! But no...! Not even a hand...! 'Cause right away they say it's the High Command.... What that mean? Truth be, all them cows and pigs, them mules, horses... all for the High Command.... I tired...! Wanna get out...! I done thinking is gonna get better, and it the same. 'Cause the Sargent a beast: no one gonna get away with a pig or cow. This morning I tie up a couple of cow, damn pretty they was. Beauties...! And almost to birthing.... Thought I get some milk for my child.... And I almost have to kill that recruit Pére, the guard who took 'em from me, say for the High Command . . . that damn High Command sure is high! I thinking of going, for sure. . . ."

A short man approaches, his clothes soaked in blood:

"Shut you mouth, man . . . ! I same as always. The noose for the skinniest. . . . We fight with them blacks . . . and pigs and cows and all . . . who knows for what . . . ! And . . . shut you damn mouth . . . ! 'Cause the devil of Sargent gonna be mad, roar . . . 'cause he got order. . . . But that damn Yosefo take it all . . . ! He swallow the cigar and ain't even left the fire, ain't even left the ash . . . me, I wanted to get me a convenience store!"

Another came along, a tall one, who had been a prisoner and had gotten rid of his sentence when the Cutting arrived:

"And me, going to my house over by Moca and they make me kill those black over there, not knowing why. I try to talk to the Sargent but he stop me right there! They orders . . . they orders. . . . Says 'cause they take some cattle! Okay . . . ! But I ain't got no cattle or the devil of nothing else . . . ! And those that has cattle, like the Herrera in Dajabón, leave you half-dead, don't give a drop o' milk when you asks. . . . Not possible, they tells you when you asks . . . not a bit of milk. Not possible! For the pigs . . . ! And then, when the blacks rob him, Don Sebusto in his house, asleep, and me tying up blacks and going wild. . . . And all for nothin' . . . ! Not a goat . . . ! 'Cause I tied up one skinny goat for making something for Mameita, my woman, and the guard stole it right off . . . ! This Devil work! Not a cent . . . and my arms dead from using the dagger from sun up . . . and all night. . . . I came here for two heifer I stole from a Spaniard in Moca . . . and they the heifer cost me most in my life . . . !"

The last one speaks, a short man and fast as a cat.

"When I get it they calls me to kill blacks, I say: I saved . . . ! And I go out with money and a cow. . . . You know! I see the storekeeper Jacqueline, have more cow than a rooster have feather . . . fat ones . . . Spanish . . . I dunno where she gets 'em. I say: 'All for me.' . . . And so I go with the guard, and leave 'em behind. And I jump the black man, who get scared 'cause he a coward. . . . And I say: 'Jacqueline, the money or you life!' An' she give me everything . . . ! And then I kill her . . . ! And I go out to the corral that use to be hers, and now I think is mine . . . ! I go out to see my cattle . . . ! Thinking I rich . . . ! I has cattle now . . . ! I don't remember the naked man he stay naked. . . . And I trick the guards in taking them to another place. All good. But when I getting to Loma de Cabrera . . . they search me there and the Captain take my gold and fill his pocket. . . . Damn! Soon I see Bacá coming along, the old prisoner, driving my cattle to the High Command. . . . There ain't no High Command, is the Captain himself! He steal everything and send it to his estate in Mao . . . ! Damn! And now we the same old fool, oxen. . . . This can't go on. . . ."

It is getting light. The crude creole pipes are burning out. The Sargent, nearby, had heard everything. Now he comes over.

"Where are the schoolteachers . . . ?" he roars.

He points to the group talking and gives the order: "Take 'em out . . . ! I'm gonna teach 'em better!"

The men line up across from the small forest. He finished them off with three shots from his pistol.

Then he looked at the rest of that troop, beaten down and without faith, martyrs just like the Haitians themselves. His Asiatic eyes red with rage, he shouted these words: "I used a pistol because they aren't Haitians . . . ! But this is how I carry out the Man's orders . . . ! Know that you should not be ashamed of this . . . ! This has to do with the High Command, and the General is the only one who needs to know what happens here, there in the Presidency! They done now . . . band of talkers . . . ! I heard it all . . . !

Daybreak began with burying the reservists who had wanted to flee. No one can flee here. This is an extermination camp. For everyone . . . !

Later they continue carrying out the orders of the High Command. They don't know who that boss is: the High Command. The High Command . . . who is it? Is it human? They are far away. They all think they are being punished. And, silently, all of them ask themselves: "Who is the High Command . . . ? Insatiable monster! Can it be he has a gullet big enough for all the border cattle? He must devour all the cows, all the horses, all the money. All the men."

7

Far from the village of Dajabón is the Castellanos palm grove. Pigs and blacks have lived on this landscape of pines and royal palms. In freedom. The blacks have worked hard, and have breeding pens and large fields. There, the hordes have also carried out their mission of extermination.

The Castellanos palm grove sings a sad song. The whispering wind can be heard beneath the pines. Song or *miserere* ...? A terrifying calm.

This is not a poetic moon. Rather, it is a moon that accuses. It shines white on more than three hundred decapitated heads that remain intact in its light along the path. The heads are of young men, old people, and women. The killers wore soldiers' uniforms and the ragged uniforms of prisoners.

That landscape made for love became a place of death. By dusk the lamentations and shrieks had died down. Everything is finished. Peace. The peace of death.

My mule jumps over the scattered skulls as if they were stones in the riverbed. I think: "And where is the soul ...? Does the soul exist ...? And consciousness ...? Does consciousness exist ...?"

The only survivors were Yosefo and his family. Yosefo was the pure-blood son of a Haitian and a black Dominican.

This is the story. When they were about to kill everyone, Sargent Pío stopped the horde of prisoners. Yosefo Dis and his daughters should be spared. Of course, these people should go to Haiti.

It is a dialogue that freezes the daggers in midair. Why? Of course: Manuelita is Dominican, and with Yosefo, the Haitian richest in crops and cattle, has given birth to a family of seven. But it isn't his wealth, stolen now, that saves Yosefo and his blacks. The prisoners have already swept his fields and sent his cows to the Captain's hacienda in Mao. It's that Manuelita the Dominican is Sargent Pío's illegitimate sister. The Sargent and Yosefo are *compadres*. The Sargent had baptized Francois, the oldest.

"... Okay ... Yosefo.... I've broken the law.... I've broken the law ... and you all get out and go on to Haiti ...! Right now ...! Get your things and your children, and get going before the others come ...!"

Yosefo has trouble understanding.... Leave Castellanos ... "his" land! When he arrived he was poor. And now he must leave that land, leave everything and go with two mules, his children, and a few household things. He must leave his money, his cows, his pigs, that were many. Now he was supposed to go to Haiti. To what? To starve.

Manuelita hasn't heard the Sargent's words and screams pitifully.

"Don't kill my sons ...! Take everything ...! What abuse! And poor Yosefo, who Dominican now ...! Just yesterday his papers come from the capital, from a Ministry ...!

"The papers say Yosefo from here now, like us ...! And the house ... and the animals ... such struggle.... What abuse! What abuse!"

"Manuelita ... Manuelita," the Sargent says. "Be quiet! Be quiet ...! You know this order from High Command ... from big boss ...! Be quiet, 'cause you a Dominican ...!"

"And my children ... and Yosefo." She spoke with anguish and determination. She wanted to flee and she also wanted to die.

Sargent Tarragona let her speak and implore. Meanwhile, he ordered his men to ready two mules and two donkeys. And he made the children, Yosefo, and Manuela mount them.

When she mounted, he said two words, tenderly: "Goodbye, sister! What can we do!" (At that moment, he seemed like a condemned man.) He cried. And he looked once more at his sister, distant now, who was heading to a country she didn't know.

The family went off toward the nearest border point, sorrowfully. But Jacmel is far away. That's where Yosefo came from, twenty years ago. He thinks: "More than 350 kilometers. Twenty years lost, clearing hardwood trees, bush, brambles on La Línea,* and getting up early every day, conquering the rains, driving the old Spanish owner's cattle—his name was Nebbott, a Catalan. And settling in Castellanos, where pigs multiply like mango leaves." Yosefo is Christian. These words escape his broad lips: *"Bon Dieu . . . ! Bon Dieu . . . !"*

This sun kills. A yellow sun, almost red, the sun of Lent. The young ones will be hungry when they wake up. Jacmel is far away and his bag is empty because Brother Santos took all his money. Brother Santos, the prisoner who was serving time in Monte Cristy for having murdered his wife, his mother-in-law, and son. Yosefo's children are headed to another land, that of his father.

The children cry in Spanish now. In Haiti, who will understand them?

AS MY MULE PLODS through the night, tripping over the skulls of this ossuary, I think about the notion of Justice. Yes, Justice. . . . My thoughts turn to my country's capital, and I can see the fat bald men, surely cowards, sitting in a cabinet meeting somewhere or other. What are these men doing? They must be examining legal codes, scrutinizing international law, thinking up schemes, and one of them might be theorizing something "new and interesting." They smoke American tobacco in their long pipes. What is it all for, in that elegant hall with its mahogany and cedar carvings? It's late at night and they work

---

* La Línea (literally, "the line") is the border between the Dominican Republic and Haiti. It also refers to the border area.

feverishly. They work to justify the strongman who established the Cutting, and forgive the barbarous assault of the Cat, Brother Santos, Sargent Tarragona, and his men.

"Justice . . ." Those who smoke Virginia tobacco know nothing of the tragic plague of lobsters on Castellanos's land. I, on the other hand, am recording the spectacle as if in an inebriated dream. Above my head, tossed randomly about like some phantasmagorical modern painting, there is a river of blood in which many heads float among plentiful pieces of fruit. In this river of my chimera, swollen cattle swim, mountains of grass go by, decapitated farmworkers, fleeing pigs, and frightened cows. And there is fire on the water, lots of fire. Smoke, lots of smoke. . . . What is this? It is an approximation of conscience. And all this is happening on an island in the Antilles divided between two countries, in each of which there is a population battered by hunger and by the whips of those who rule.

Where am I going . . . ? I myself do not know, as the mule continues along its way. "What am I looking for here?" my conscience asks. "Why are you still here . . . ? Why don't you leave . . . ? You are hungry, like these dead . . . but the bread you eat is stained with blood. . . . If you stay, you too will be floating in that river, that river of blood!!!"

And all I hear is the murmur of the pines, the far-off barking of dogs.

Once again, I think of the pudgy men who right now are working on new international schemes. I also think of my country's journalists, tied to oppression's wagon, who write the stories about this event they haven't witnessed. News that lies.

And the journalist knows he lies, that he is going against his conscience. Perhaps on the front page of tomorrow's paper, he will write: *"There is peace on La Línea. There have only been isolated incidents between a few landowners and the Haitian thieves."* (That reporter has never been to Castellanos.) He would tremble if he spoke with a drunk Sargent or prisoner at a dance in the village of Capotillo. There, Sargent Tarragona, great accordionist that he is, plays the *juangomero*, a vibrant music of the Northwest Line, and might speak to him of the decapitated with the same sporting calm as a university student enthusiastically recounting his victories on the volleyball field.

On any given day, since the Cutting began, a strange head might show up in the plaza of some Haitian village. This might coincide with an act of "Dominican-Haitian friendship," beginning with a diplomatic toast. Diplomats are fine men. They love peace. They explain peace. The diplomats will raise their glasses to the deepest friendship between the two peoples. (Now I am thinking of the prisoners: they have been freed from their sentences by the Cutting. Now I am the prisoner.)

8

The old white man with his gangly beard looked like a Quixote among all those blacks. The house was perfect for the desert, a simple one of solid construction. After the solemnity with which General Guilito Pichardo, head of the Lilís regiment, and Demetrio Rodríguez on other occasions, arrived at his home, old man Miguel Bueno set about to deal with the massacre. He made a late attempt to save the lives of a few blacks who were like his own children, house servants and those who waited on his wife. He knew it wouldn't be long before the prisoners led by Sargent Pío arrived. This man, who barely knew how to write but whose cattle negotiations sealed by his word were underwritten by the greatest dignity, had to lay low now. To save lives.

That was a sad landscape, whose homes nonetheless offered gracious smiles to their visitors. One could see the big house from a distance, standing on stilts made of *calderón*, an especially hard wood found along the frontier. Its roof was made of cane, a fiber that grows in dry climates, that seemed to have been woven by angels.

Captain Bijo's troops had consummated their usual acts of barbary. Miguel Bueno had buried all his blacks. Old man Lembé hadn't been able to escape. The old-timers of the village had hidden him. But damned be one prisoner's astuteness. The Cat, as he was called, found the old man and made him his most defenseless victim. When they departed, they left Miguel Bueno's house in shadows, replete with repressed tears.

Now it was another armed retinue. They arrived at Miguel Bueno's house, searching for more blacks. Someone may have betrayed him.

It's a difficult situation. The black girls had taken refuge in the bedroom of Miguel Bueno's wife. But now he had made up his mind. They would have to kill him first.

"Sargent, come in, but only you . . . ! I don't want my home dirtied by criminal hordes . . . ! No soldiers, either . . . ! Great men have come to this house, like Demetrio Guelito . . . but criminals, no . . . ! Step back, or kill me if you must."

Some of the soldiers want to enter and attempt to do so, but Don Miguel threatens them. His only weapon is his old cane, a gift from General Demetrio Rodríguez, and these days he has more character than strength. The old man's character half restrains the prisoners whose daggers are unsheathed.

Step back, he threatens. The prisoners hesitate. They know who Miguel Bueno is: a prestigious gentleman, a man who has given everything to the poor. Some are afraid. That is why they hesitate.

Then a lion's voice intervenes. It's Sargent Tarragona.

"Get back! Swine! Evil ones! Don't you know who this is? Who dares lift a hand to this old man . . . ! Get back!"

And they all put their daggers away.

Don Miguel seemed like a condemned man. He was livid. With his cane raised, he resembled a statue. Rigid and mute. A tempest raged in his head then. To him, love of his neighbor was worth more than death. He had made up his mind: he must die with the last of the blacks. Now he barely noticed Sargent Pío approaching him, humble as a dog, who remembered what Don Miguel had done for his poor widowed mother and all her children. At this moment, Don Miguel also made him think of scenes from the civil war so many years before. The old man had torn him from the post to which he had been tied by the revolutionaries, rescuing him moments before the troop's rifles would have put an end to his life.

In that instant, that other earlier moment flashed before his eyes. After the rain. The firefight had ended, and he was wounded when they'd captured him. A southern chief, who was with the rebel troop, said: "This one first, because he's the bravest." He was already tied to the post. "Tie him good, and may he place himself in God's hands!" shouted the chief. But at that moment Don Miguel Bueno arrived to save him from the firing squad. The chief accepted money from Don Miguel and left him there, untied him from the stake, and brought him home, to this very house where right now this furious band of prisoners had come to search, seize, and slit the throats of hidden blacks.

"Back off, swine, get out! Wait for me on the road!"

They obeyed his orders. And now Don Miguel returns to the living. He embraces Pío and, stammering, says: "My son . . . what is this?! Why are you mixed up in this . . . ? Why . . . ? A brave man like you . . . how did you get involved in this coward's work . . . ?"

They had to help the old man, whose heart had all but given out. As he accommodates him in the great rocking chair, Sargent Pío consoles Don Miguel: "They're gone . . . Don Miguel, those swine . . . ! It's all right. They won't kill another black man here! Over my dead body. They're gone! The High Command will have to execute me first!"

Later he drank a cup of coffee and calmly reminisced about times gone by.

"Don't you remember, Don Miguel . . . when I ruled here . . . and the day General Demetrio came round . . . and the time they had me tied to the post and you gave me back my life . . . ! Ay, Don Miguel . . . always such a good man . . . and when my leg was rotting and your wife, Mistress Micaela, saved me. . . . You remember when you rescued me from the hands of Toño Jorge, when they were gonna shoot me? You're a daddy to me, and I don't know who my daddy was. . . . You're my daddy!"

Don Miguel was quiet and the Sargent went on.

"And this . . . this morning . . . it was government orders . . . the big bosses . . . the biggest boss of all, Don Miguel . . . ! What you gonna do . . . ? That black want to conquer the Republic . . . and they all thieves, Don Miguel . . . they even come for you . . . !"

Strange tears glistened in those beasts' eyes. He fell silent. He looked up at the moon, high among the pines, and then left with his men, who hadn't understood a word.

"Eh, God . . . ! Poor now, like a beggar . . . and still his hand open. . . . No one around here ever know who that man is. . . . All this land belong to him. . . . And this weren't more than a few cattle and whatever animal God create. . . . And the revolutionaries done finish it all. . . . But his hand still open, willing to die to save them blacks he raise like his own children. . . . No . . . no . . . ! I ain't gonna carry out Captain Windbag's orders. In Don Miguel's house I ain't going! Let 'em shoot me tomorrow! It okay with me! But why don't the General make war on Haiti . . . ? I ashamed to kill these people. . . . I like to fight like the revolutionaries . . . ! The troops with their commander, with their bugle and flag . . . ! Why don't we take Haiti . . . ?"

No one speaks. No one understands. No one dares contradict him. He is the most dangerous of these beasts. Night consumes fifty gallows faces.

9

Long white roads, as if dusted with wheat. If the crime had its hours, like a work day that begins at dawn and ends at dusk, these would surely not be the most appropriate. At night, the moon speaks to the soul. Still warm from sleep, the savannah rests on its sheets of translucent mist. Everything appears to sleep beneath the moon's wheat.

The men keep walking. There isn't a black to be seen. Where are they? Have they all fled? Have they already crossed El Masacre?

They haven't fled. They lay dead beneath the brush. Captain Bijo, that guy with little Asian eyes, had preceded Sargent Pío.

The pigs rooting around revealed the macabre scene. A silvery moon illuminated hundreds of heads strewn about the savannah where those animals roamed. And the guide dog ran with what they found. Behind came a pack of other dogs. Leg bones were scattered on the road. It seems like walking is Haiti's destiny. Between the teeth of pigs and dogs now. The Haitian is a black gypsy beneath a Caribbean sky. His destiny is to walk: to flee his country and all its lashes, like in olden times when it was a French plantation, producer of coffee, sugar, and indigo for colonial enrichment. Now they flee from the large landowners, an exotic people. Why do they come to Santo Domingo . . . ? For land . . . ? Do they look for a new place in which to exercise the most basic of all rights: to live? But there will be no end to this march. After the massacre, their skinny legs travel on in the mouths of pigs and dogs.

PATRICIO, THE RECRUIT, had been born poor. Poor child, poor youth. Poor man. Why do others have things and he not . . . ? At this tragic party, he was thirsty for gold. He observed the Sargent stealing cattle and coins. But there was nothing for him, just as there was nothing for the prisoners or the reservists. Now he thinks about looking for gold in El Almácigo, where there are rich Haitians who bought gold from those who panned for it in the rivers.

This thought brings him to hide in the small forest, to separate himself from the troop that goes on ahead.

Patricio, the recruit, is alone now, beneath what's left of the moon. He is going to argue with the dogs. Let them eat the corpses . . . but he will search for gold among the dead. Patricio, the recruit, is a deranged soul. He seems to have gone mad on these death marches. He figures out how to ply gold teeth from the dead.

Barbarous obsession!

Despite his madness, he seems to tremble, but now he is fully engaged in his machinations. He will search the mouths of the dead! In the cities too there are ghoulish thieves who rob tombs.

He was sitting under the trees with a head in his hands. He was trembling.

This head . . . is it trying to laugh? And he trembles. By the moon's light, he observes it, and observes it again. Is the head going to bite him . . . ? Ay, and he tosses it aside. "Damned farmhand . . . ," he cries, to calm his own fear. The head has no gold! And he tosses it. Now another. . . . It is frozen in its rictus. With difficulty, he pries open the jaw! Nothing there either . . . ! And he tosses it. That one will have something! It's big, must have been some rich merchant. He parts the jaw and finds nothing.

Dawn arrives. Now a dog stalks him, a tattletale witness. Irritated, he tosses the last head away, and the dog's bark rouses his ire. . . . But there is no gold!

The madman looks awkward, like some drunk in this ossuary. Could the gold be a lie . . . ? But no, he says. . . . It's somewhere on this savannah, hidden in belts, in jackets, hidden before Captain Bijo's arrival . . . and he runs here and there. He doesn't find gold. Those damned prisoners talking about gold! It's a lie. He will get revenge!

Morning finds him exhausted. He is alone. He's without a mount, because his mule wandered off, far off, across the plains. And now . . . ? He thinks about the Sargent's punishment. He is alone now, crazy and dirty. He thinks of El Almácigo again. He will go to El Pino, another village. That's where he'll find his fortune. He'll bring in the harvest with the blacks. He thinks he will go on ahead. When he gets to El Pino, he'll rob the home of Isaías Ten, the guy who buys cattle and got a prize two months ago. . . . That one has money . . . !

This time the Sargent will be late . . . and I'll get the Moors . . . !

He catches sight of El Pino in the distance. He thinks: Has the Sargent already gotten there? He imagines what he will do with the Haitian's cattle. . . . The best thing would be to hide them in the mountains, or sell them in Dajabón. . . . But what if the Captain is in Dajabón . . . ? He owns all the cows. . . . What will happen . . . ? Ah, yes, at Isaías's house . . . but . . . where is his knife . . . ? It's not here. . . . Where did he leave it . . . ? He must have left it on the savannah when he was searching through the corpses. How stupid he is! And what will he do . . . ?

Patricio, the recruit, was desperate. He thought about hiding then. Or maybe he should flee . . . yes, flee . . . ! Dress like a peasant and flee! Where . . . ? Far, far away, until they confuse him with a Haitian so another patrol will kill him. . . . But . . . flee . . . flee . . . ! He thinks: "Damn poverty . . . and before I became a guard I was a good shoe-maker. . . . I didn't earn much but . . . I was better off!"

Then he began to run . . . ! He took off his military shirt. He threw it away and kept running. Across the vast plain. The madman fled, running faster all the time.

A patrol picked him up and dragged him, raving, before the Sargent.

"I'm going...! I'm going...! I'm going...!" It was all he managed to say.

The Sargent faced the madman: "Shut this man up...! I never believed in the people from Sui... they fled like chickens! They say they want money... asking for a mule and a coat of skins...! He gonna pay...! 'Cause a mule's worth more than a coward here...!"

THE MESSAGE SENT TO THE CAPTAIN, along with a bunch of bedraggled parrots, written in the bush by the only soldier who knew how to write, said: "To inform you, my Captain... the recruit Patricio run off like a scared rooster and end up crazy.... With luck say whatever. With respect, Sargent Tarragona."

When no one was looking, Patricio, the recruit, the madman, escaped. There he goes, running back and forth across the savannah. Where is he going...? He is fleeing, fleeing.

10

In El Almácigo, in the hills, wrapped in his sheath of banana leaves, paralytic and blind. In his youth, in Haiti, he'd been an elementary schoolteacher. What happened to Mustalí Dois in his country, nobody knows, but he's lived for more than fifty years on Dominican soil. The old man speaks half in Patois, half in Spanish, especially when he spends time with his grandchildren.

"*Christophe le roi* . . . ! Big man . . . bigger than all Dominicans . . . once Dessalines killed two thousand whites in El Cabo. . . . *Et le empereur Soulouque . . . et Toussaint . . .*"

No one can understand him. He half walks, feeling his way as if he can see, and tries to find out where Haiti is. Mustalí is afraid of Juan Nazario, the Dominican married to his daughter. When Juan is at work, he dares whisper a threat intended to put light in his dulled eyes:

"*Dominiquén. . . . Dominiquén. . . . Pas vaut. . . . Dominiquén ne travails pas. . . . Dominiquén, voleur. . . . Vive le noire Toussaint . . . ! Vive Toussaint Louverture!*"

Mustalí remembers his years as a rural teacher, before the Dominican forest swallowed him up.

Then it seems like the blacks of his dead eyes see the stars, the high and brilliant stars of La Línea, spread profusely across the blue of a cool night. Mustalí curls up and remembers that Haiti controlled the Dominicans for many years. How many . . . ? He can't remember, but a lot.

"No speak Spanish. . . . *Pití . . . ne pale pañol, pití . . . tu soy jaitién . . .*"

The children don't understand him. The old man is in the corner caressing old dreams—of imperial Haiti—and utters a stereotypical phrase, learned in school in his youth, Haiti's official phrase: "*Une et indivisible . . .*" And he falls silent.

"*Dominiquén pas vaut. . . .*" He's always thought this, as long as he's lived as a Dominican on land not his. "*Dominiquén pas vaut . . . ,*" as he worked as a slave for the mulatto boss of Santiago de la Cruz, laboring in the still or in the cane fields, or driving cattle from Dajabón to Puerto Plata . . .

One day, when Juan Nazario, his daughter's Dominican mate, reproached him that Haitians are "mangy dogs," he didn't answer but muttered in a low voice: "*Toussaint va vuelva pa mandá dominiquén . . . !*" (Toussaint is coming back to rule over the Dominicans.)

But Juan Nazario, the Dominican, didn't understand these words. Now the blood of Dominicans is in Mustalí's house. And the old man is useless at the ranch. His daughter, Juan Nazario's woman, didn't know, like Mustalí did, who Toussaint was. But she hated Dominicans.

For his part, her husband, Juan Nazario, in moments of anger, especially when the Haitians steal his crops or his cattle, roars: "Damn blacks . . . ! Kill 'em all . . . ! Get rid of them for good . . . ! Even the small ones . . . all of 'em gone . . . ! Ain't worth planting . . . they steal everything. . . . And me, Dominican, I leave my country to take up with these dirty black, they smell like dead birds! I can't wait to go to war with Haiti, so we can cut off heads and rip bellies all the way to Port-au-Prince . . . finish that damn race off once and for all! And I sure Jeremi a thief, that brother of the black Haitian mother of my kids. . . . He stole from me, even though he know I work for his nephew, these mixed-bloods, children of me and the Haitian. They no good! Stinking race!"

Old man Mustalí listened and said nothing. But he thought: "*Dominiquén pas vaut.*"

Juan Nazario went back to his escapades: "Better the devil have his rights already. Shit . . . ! The day the government get involved in this, even the purebloods gonna go!"

In El Almácigo he is pensive. Listening to the words that sound at Juan Nazario's ranch, beside the coffee grove, he seems to listen, intervene.

Two people, two separate entities, on one precious little green island in the Caribbean. The faint beat of a distant drum can be heard. In the patio, Juan Nazario's sons speak Patois. And Juan Nazario goes out into the patio and shouts at them: "Fuckin' race . . . ! Race of thieves . . . ! Speak Spanish!" And the purebloods speak Spanish.

WHEN THE PRISONERS GOT to El Almácigo, the miserable shacks were still sleeping. This is a swatch of human misery on a moonlit landscape. At the only inn on the road, there is a beautiful innkeeper—her skin all plum and cinnamon. A roadway with a yellow sun, a Lenten sun, seeps through the door. After a fiesta of pine trees, the shacks look like rats, nestled in the dew. In the straw houses, whitened with lime, there are deep breaths, strong odors. Why is it? Black loves white: lime for the houses. Or dirty red, swept with a coarse broom, hard like the bickering of those who paint.

Catlin Dass shouted loud for the Cat, the prisoner. . . . She shouted and jumped up and down and even charged the drunk assassin, who emitted a frightening guffaw.

Catlin Dass woke the village and already the blacks were fleeing across the plain like Guinea fowl.

"Attack! Attack!"

"Negresses one way, men the other!" the Sargent shouted. And then, even louder: "If you have a place, get going quickly! No time to lose!"

"Sargent, pardon, I don't have nothing . . . !"

Everyone in the village died. Then another infernal shriek was heard, in Spanish. It was the purebloods, Juan Nazario's children.

"Don't kill us, we Dominicans . . . ! *Nu sóm dominiquén . . . semo domincanos . . . Dominiquén . . .* !"

"Take the cow. . . . Save me . . . ! I *dominiquén . . .* !"

"Take it all, *soy dominiquén . . .* !"

"I *dominicano . . . dominiquén . . .* ! I never been to Haiti, born here!"

"I from here . . . my country *dominiquén.* Grew up in Dajabón!"

"Damn! They gonna kill the Dominicans?"

It was Juan Nazario's authoritative voice that halted the troop. Then the Sargent recognized Juan Nazario, the Dominican, the brave one, the one who had been his comrade in the revolution, at Cerro de las Mercedes.

"Halt! Stop there! Halt!" he shouted energetically, stopping the prisoners who were about to fall upon Juan Nazario, who met them with his machete raised, ready to fight.

"Damn, Juan Nazario! Juan Nazario!" he repeated, as he embraced him warmly.

"And you, what you doing in these hills, with all this Haitians? What you doing with all this swine . . . ? A real man, like yourself? Speak, Juan . . . !"

"These blacks my sons!" Juan Nazario said. "And I sorry . . . ! I left everything to go to the hills to plant coffee and . . . But, what I gonna do in the hills . . . ? Man can't even find a whore here . . . and this sun and hunger, take a week clearing trees, an' you don't know what you doing! Then a man take a dog of a woman. . . . I clearing land with that old man Mustalí, paralytic, and I took his daughter to cook. And the negress came down with child. Liken that . . . and up in the hill with those mangy folk, I become a Haitian dog. You can see, can't no way talk right, or guards take me for a *mañé.*"

He stopped talking. Then added: "Forgive these black . . . ! My children they are! Even half-Haitian! Do it for your Lieutenant Juan Nazario! Remember?"

The Sargent meditated. It was true. This was Juan Nazario, his comrade from the revolution. Juan Nazario, brave among the brave.

"Comrade Nazario . . . ! Comrade Nazario . . . ! You gone join the wrong band! A man like you, should be officer in the Guard, 'cause you pulse don't tremble, I know you . . . ! Hiding out in these hill like *mañé*! Shit! Jesus Christ!! Give me something. . . . Take me where they are!"

Juan Nazario, who knows how poor his blacks are, answers resolutely: "Comrade Pío . . . ! Not even a dog afraid here . . . ! You gonna have to kill us all, but me first! 'cause I want to die at peace with you . . . ! And if I see you kill a black woman, even if she Haitian, I gotta curse you good. That's right, and you know me!"

Faced with that challenge, the Sargent became agitated. He knows who Juan Nazario is. He knows Juan Nazario's valor. The prisoners await his orders. The purebloods tremble. There is a profound silence. Some murmur a prayer, softly, almost unintelligibly. Others say: "*Nou som dominiquén . . .*"

Standing tall, Juan Nazario, tells them: "Shut up, mangy dogs!"

"Let it be . . . ! Come on!" He has the machete in his hand, ready to fight. Sargent Pío remains silent; he doesn't know what to do. Finally, he says these words, slowly, almost bitterly: "Juan Nazario . . . ! Get on, go with all these blacks to Haiti! Take 'em . . . and go back to your country . . . ! 'Cause you're one of the good Dominicans!"

Juan Nazario lowers his sword and responds: "I stay there . . . 'cause I now another mangy dog!"

And so Juan Nazario's family leaves for Haiti. Blind Mustalí, the old teacher, on his gentle burro. Behind are the hills, ownerless land replete with coffee plants swollen with red berries that will fall to the ground with no one to harvest them.

On the journey, nobody speaks. Juan Nazario brings up the rear, guiding his troop of mangy dogs, as he calls them.

When one of his sons speaks in Patois, his commanding voice can be heard: "Damn dog . . . ! Speak Spanish . . . !"

11

The school was a broken-down shack. The school at El Almácigo. Its students were mostly the sons and daughters of Haitians. There were also *catizos*—children of Haitians and Dominicans, or vice versa. On the ugly landscape, the teacher provided contrast: she was pretty. And that was dangerous for a woman, to be a teacher, which basically means you are miserable, and to be pretty, something that incites the sadism of one of the many savages who live on this far-off land. The girl was barely twenty years old and from the South. She had cinnamon-colored skin and greenish eyes. Beautiful black braids and a figure worthy of a model in one of the aristocratic fashion houses to be found in any great city. But she was a rural schoolteacher. Poverty: the word that says it all in this country.

This teacher, Angela Vargas, had wanted to leave her hometown—Azua—go to the university, and get a pharmacy degree. In Santo Domingo, women who aren't interested in fashion magazines, recipes, and the latest styles, but are determined to involve themselves in an intellectual pursuit, choose pharmacy. But this poor girl's university dreams were doomed by her father's death. She became a rural school-teacher in the fields outside Azua, where she lived with her mother. So as to keep her dignity, the girl had accepted the countryside's rudeness.

One day, an order from the Ministry of Education, a capricious order as all those from that department were, sent her to the distant frontier to impart classes to the blacks of Haitian origin, the new serfs who, since they had penetrated our lands, now had to be considered Dominicans because they were born on our soil. And Angela Vargas went off. Now she works on the brown lands of El Almácigo, a wild place and lonely, where she—the teacher—is the only person who knows such a thing as a *Dominican Republic* exists. What's that, the surprised inhabitants of the place would ask, who only possess their miserable lives, like those of pigs, with no notion of homeland.

The students were blacks: barefoot, half-naked, hungry. The circulars—the orders and instructions coming down from the Ministry of Education—demanded a thousand affectations and requirements regarding clothing, school supplies, books, and so forth, with which those "students" were supposed to comply.

The teacher thought: "How do I demand school uniforms from those who only have rags, like their parents . . ." And so the teacher makes no requirements and simply offers her classes to the half-naked children.

One day the Inspector arrived. The Inspector was a man who had also been a teacher once, and had risen through the ranks. The Inspector had dreams of bettering himself. He would go far. And to do that, he must demonstrate a lot of zeal to the Ministry. He must be very demanding!

The Inspector reprimanded the teacher for not having carried out the orders in circulars number fifteen and twenty . . . among others. . . . Then he got back on his mule and disappeared on the savannah. The Inspector left happy: the teacher in El Almácigo had given him reason to denounce her. . . . What's more, he had taken her to his bed and then tossed her aside. . . . He had shown his zeal, thus accumulating merits that would allow him to rise in the system. Perhaps one day he would get to be Under Secretary or, why not, with the aid of a great lady in the town where the President spent the night when he visited the border, even Minister of Education himself . . . !

The "dossier" against the teacher in El Almácigo was quick to follow. To defend herself and try to keep her job, she traveled to the capital. In the end, she saved her miserable position. The Department understood the scarcity suffered by the inhabitants of El Almácigo, whose poverty made it impossible for them to have proper clothing. It was a distant land, dry, without roads, without stores, destitute. Only high country, vast plains, solitude. The Minister barely raised his eyes to look at the teacher, but in the end, he accepted her explanation. That's La Línea. There is hunger and thirst there. And the fat Minister, puffing on his Havana cigar, ended up forgiving the young teacher's "crime." She had spent a month's salary on this trip. But . . . she had to defend herself against the Inspector!

As she left the building, a chubby-cheeked man, with round glasses, sitting in his car, sent his chauffeur to "invite her to take a drive . . . visit his country house. . . ." This is a frequent offer when it comes to pretty, poor women. But the young teacher had abundant dignity. She thought about herself, about her mother. She looked at her outfit, bleached by the sun of those plains. She looked at her unfashionable shoes, despite which she was acceptable looking. She thought of her poverty and refused the fat man who had spotted her from behind the window of his luxurious silver automobile adorned with its official license plate: *"Under Secretary."*

As she fled the lecher's vulgar sight—he seemed like a fatty beast behind the window of his car—she thought of the El Almácigo plains: there is poverty there, but also freedom. The gluttonous Under Secretary never goes there. He doesn't know La Línea. There she is safe from these criminals. And she has the hope of bringing some light to the souls of those country people who are now learning how to speak decent Spanish, those she hopes to be able to make understand what the Dominican Republic is.

BACK IN EL ALMÁCIGO. Naked children. Miserable salary. But the teacher feels more at home than in the city with all its deceits. From her window, she looks out upon the great prairie. She's always afraid of seeing the Inspector's mule. Until he comes, she is free to create nationhood. She is isolated from the rest of the country. Sometimes a newspaper arrives, always late. In the most recent, the teacher found a long speech by the fat Minister: it was a lengthy defense of "the Father of the New Dominican School."*

One day the teacher received unexpected news. The school would close the following month. The teacher would lose her job. But there wouldn't be time for all that. "The Cutting" arrived that very morning at the doors of the El Almácigo school. The teacher woke to the blacks' desperate cries.

Horrified, Angela Vargas witnesses the massacre. Like a tree chopped down, she saw the body of gentle black Samuel, the water carrier, fall to the ground. She taught his children. Carlos Almonte, a prisoner who'd been serving time on La Línea for his crimes in Puerto Plata, was freed now by government order, and thousands of delinquents like him brandished arms and daggers in a horrendous harvesting of heads! She also saw Daniel, the carpenter who had fashioned the school's rustic desks, mowed down after shouting, imploring, his right to a poor man's life on the hard earth that now served as his final resting place beneath a torrid sun.

What to do . . . ? Shout, beg! Nothing. Her books and entreaties lost themselves in the hellish spectacle of the green savannah that had become red. But now the mob was going for the cornered children! And she could resist no longer! She lost consciousness, like a mad woman, calling out to God! Yes, God! A God that belonged to everyone, without distinction of skin color or national origin! God! Everyone's God! And she suffered a profound vertigo. When she came to, she wailed. What did her eyes behold? Mountains of corpses!

The teacher called out in humanity's name. It was then that Captain Windbag, also drunk, arrived at the schoolhouse door, looking for another group of Haitians she had hidden in the classroom. He

---

* Trujillo took credit for all public works, all the country's development.

stopped. The drunken Captain remembered he had a crush on the teacher, who had never said a word to him.

The mob stopped outside the school door! The military men, the homicidal prisoners dressed in blue, among them the Cat and the Bacá* in the lead. The teacher implored at the Captain's feet. What happened next? No one can explain it. The Captain left with his mob.

After they were gone, the teacher let the blacks out. Under the protection of night, they fled to Haiti, crossing the border.

BUT AFTER THAT BLOODBATH, the final month was up. Now the teacher, who had lost her job, had no alternative but to leave. Where will she go? She doesn't know. If she begs the Inspector, she might be able to keep her job. The Inspector also wanted the teacher, who is pretty. She, for her part, knows the drama lying in wait for beauty and poverty in the city. In the city, there were many men who would lay their clever traps for her. But she would face her destiny boldly. She leaves. The school is empty now, penetrated by rain. Disrobed by wind. Silent and empty, like the immense savannah.

ON HER RETURN, after visiting me in Dajabón, the teacher arrived at Monte Cristy. As she was waiting for a dilapidated old bus to take her to Santo Domingo, the Inspector happened by. The man sidled up to the unemployed teacher and whispered these words: "If you stay here a few days, I'll give you work.... The President is expected to-morrow.... The President is a very good man ... and pretty women like you get everything from him...."†

At that moment, the teacher felt utter disgust for the bureaucrat. She jumped on the bus and left.

---

* Bacá is a person who, through sorcery, has been transformed into an animal, much like a shapeshifter in U.S. Indian legend.
† Trujillo was infamous for ravaging women.

When the young woman began to moan, the passengers on the bus looked at her in surprise.

"What's wrong with her?" they asked one another. Then one in the know told another: "That's the teacher from El Almácigo. They threw her out because she wouldn't go with Captain Windbag . . . !"

The other passenger, between vulgarity and disbelief, said: "Women are dumb! Look at her, so pretty, crying about a teacher's job. . . . If she wanted, she could get anything she set her heart on . . . if she went to see the President!"

The old bus continued along its way to Santiago.

12

Avoiding a fiery sun, beneath this lush tree where we sometimes take our siesta, I think about Haiti's agony, a country spurned to this day by Dominican blacks, who consider it inferior and cowardly. For their part, the Haitian has replaced the creole in market competition, working harder for less money. His is almost the life of an animal, filled with want, sustained by the sugarcane he manages to eat during the harvests undertaken by the sugar monopolies. Re-creating scenes of slavery, those companies pay Haitian minsters and other esteemed citizens, who trade in their own brothers, fifteen pesos a head for every Haitian cane cutter. This is the reappearance of black skin trade in the century of light.

We look at these immense fields along the border and a question assaults us: Who does this land belong to . . . ? Long since abandoned. Then cultivated by Haiti, that filled it with farms and fruit groves—coffee, avocados, mangoes, shade—and now desolate, plagued by crime. Why . . . ? Who will come to overexploit these abandoned coffee crops, these empty prairies . . . ?

The Dominicans were almost able to keep their ownership of the land. The revolution barely touched them. After the Conquest with its monastic colonial crosses, isolation kept these regions far from the nation's sight. Revolutionary ideas reached Juan Calvo, Cerro de las Mercedes, Chacuey, La Guajaca. Only with the Restoration did Dominican soldiers reach these hills. The dead remained, and then eternal silence.

The loneliness of these noble and deserving lands, tomb to so many generations lost to rebels on one side or another. Great cattle-grazing lands, only a stain now, fertilized day after day, while in Dajabón important men napped, smoked long cigars or slow pipes in houses whose architecture resembled a Senegalese kiosk. At night, the village was without light. A big moon was its only illumination, and always those clear stars above the ancient Marién fiefdom.

Revolutionary history is tragic in these lands. Generations of men of every race, mowed down by civil war. The mutilated, the invalids, could not be taken to hospitals and were left on the savannah to die. Cattle were decimated. The rebels carried nothing but salt. Hundreds of cooking fires for meat appeared on the plains. The rebels, who fought without pay, ate meat they stole on the savannah. But the cattle multiplied again at a pace that made lazy masters into rich men, who worked the land with Haitian shepherds. These are the blacks who have now been hunted down on these dark lands fertilized with blood.

At night, the town of Dajabón is silent and dark. The swift savannah wind reaches town and with it the sound of dogs. From Chacuey, from Beller, desolate fields where Haitians are dying again, just as in our liberation wars. On that savannah, we freed ourselves from the chains with which Haiti subjugated the Dominican Republic for twenty-two years. During that time Haiti decapitated, shot, and piteously harassed the Dominican people. And today's daggers . . . ?

For seven days, the massacre has invaded villages and fields, hills and lowlands. Haiti is falling apart, strewn with children's belongings, chickens, and items of first necessity, crossing the international border in terror, crossing the small river called El Masacre.

Just as we've gathered our mules, Sargent Tarragona's troop shows up. As he goes by, he waves and says: "Go with God . . . ! We're going to the hills! The Haitian is a tick that has befallen the Republic, and we must kill the last tick! Farewell!"

An immense herd appears, driven by prisoners and reservists. Cows, bulls and robust heifers born along the way. When someone asked where they were taking all those cattle, the prisoner who was acting as a guide called out: "We're taking these cattle to Mao . . . ! To Captain Windbag's farm. The Cappy owns all the cattle . . . !!"

And he smiled, lopsidedly, sarcastic and sad.

13

The leaves of that beautiful tree called the *chachá* fall profusely. That's how Haiti fell. Haiti traded hearts for mangoes.

Each mango is worth a heart. Hearts are like mangoes. The breeze felled mangoes for the pigs who devour them, or they're crushed by mules' hooves; passersby don't even notice them. That same breeze kicks up Haiti's hunger, and each mango costs a heart. Haiti is dying like the fruit beneath a full moon, the fruit its people planted on Dominican land abandoned by Dominicans.

The Dominican soldiers ignore the fruit because this land doesn't feed them. The Dominican state feeds them with miserable salaries. But the soldier is happy. The soldier pays no attention to the mangoes or avocados. Rather, he murders the black who took a few mangoes from his plot of land after an endless march through the dark night.

On La Línea, there is a strange scale of human values. A cow is worth more than a prisoner and a Haitian less than a mango. A terrible sun burns. The breeze shines copper or polishes ebony. In the capitals, they speak of peace. A few magazines advertise the "prosperity" of the Antilles, while on that land the creole ranchers can't raise a cow because Haiti, searching for yucca or meat, will steal it in the night. Tragedy compels the Haitian to play a dangerous hand: rape La Línea. In his country, the farmers have no land. And the drought put an end to his farming opportunities in a country whose abrupt topography—almost entirely mountainous—barely offers the hope of a decent harvest. And so hunger pushes that impoverished people to cross La Línea. A furtive march of hunger, on which each fruit is paid for with a red heart.

In the cities, they are barely conscious of this. The sagacious diplomats don't mention it either; with their long Havana cigars, they advocate for longer siestas, reminisce about Paris, and speak of "the war in Europe."

For many years, Haiti sowed Dominican land. Now it wanted to return for the harvest. Hunger. On the great estates, the laborers were from Haiti—cheap labor. These shepherds, displaced to Haiti, returned now to the abandoned Dominican haciendas to steal the very cattle they'd cared for as if they belonged to their own family.

IF A MANGO COSTS a heart, a calf is worth twice as much. The proportional estimate confuses a hungry man. And to get one bull, it's necessary to take the lot. When he's made it through forty kilometers of hills and valleys under the cloak of night with its diamond display of stars, the black man may have arrived at El Masacre alive. He may have managed to avoid the patrols that pardon no one. It is a death card. Its other face is life. It is Haiti's hunger that plunders at night. The final effort is required at El Masacre, that shallow border river. The driven cattle drink their last Dominican water and leave their dung to fertilize the bush. If a dagger emerging from the shadows doesn't silently kill the black shepherd, the next morning the Haitian butcher will have a lot of work. The hungry Haitian got his meat!

ALONG THE WAY, a thousand heavy footprints. A rude pattern of hooves: those of cattle and of blacks. The cattle had been stolen very far away—more than forty kilometers—from Las Matas de Santa Cruz. The shepherds came from even farther away—from La Alcahie. They had crossed El Masacre. And they had returned on successive nights. The farm dogs didn't bark. Why? It's a mystery. They made off with all the cattle!

"The Devil get me . . . ! Can't live no more . . . ! Weren't no use to kill the negress big with child . . . ! These Haitian worse than disgrace themself . . . ! We gotta go on the other side . . . to Santiago, where you can raise a cow or pig . . . and after all this work . . . ! And they make off with all the cows . . . !"

"*Taíta* . . . ! *Taíta* . . . !" says Ezequiel Miolán, refilling his pipe at dusk: "This land is bitter. . . . We have to leave it . . . ! Is a witch's work. . . . I slept in that corral . . . and the dogs didn't bark! Virgen!"

14

The corrals emptied out. The Haitian is a nightwalker. And the breeze is his best signpost. The Haitians' noses seem to milk the air so it will tell them where the corrals are. The stench of manure gives them away in the night. The thief's map operates in the dark, with the breeze as its accomplice. An ABC of smells, read by a primitive race. El Patú was a good cattle foreman. He could satisfy his hungers and those of his children, who are now in Haiti on the other side of the border. His young son, Tusent, tenses from hunger on the bed of leaves since the Cutting began. El Patú sleeps during the day, and at night returns to the Dominican Republic.

The black man seemed magical. He had gone to Mole de San Nicolás to see a *bocó*, a kind of magician or fortuneteller. The *bocó* would kill the soldier who had been hunting him on the banks of El Masacre, along the narrow trails with barely room for a cow or a man. The *bocó* had said that the soldier would die and El Patú and his herd would make it to Haiti alive. El Patú learned the songs for refuge and the hex for the soldiers who guarded the international river. And, astonishingly, the animals couldn't resist. They followed him as if on their way to greener pastures.

El Patú. That's what Sargent Almonte called him. The Sargent had been watching for him without luck for fifteen nights, while he emptied fifteen hacienda corrals, all the way from La Guajaca, where there was a rifle, to Las Matas de Santa Cruz, where there were daggers supplied for the Cutting: dried blood on the poison leaf, left expressly to kill Haiti. He called him Patú because of the impression his foot left in the sands of the river. A Haitian foot, like a cow's, is a hoof; and Hilarión's was oversized. His footprint in the sand was unmistakable. And yet his machine gun was useless. That *bocó's* hex!

When the river smoothed the sand to continue carrying it on its current, it seemed to prepare a place for the thief to leave his footprint. The sand was white and well ironed, like a sheet. The soldiers' eyes kept watch. No one passes. The breeze speaks. It is late now. Some clouds appear, like the wings of black birds, and they cover the moon. El Patú went by at precisely that moment! Rifles and the machine gun were no match for him! They search for the shepherd in nearby forests filled with soldiers. He is far away by now.

The cattle are being driven across Haiti's dry lands. Now the moon reappears once more, as if laughing at the soldiers! The wet print can be seen in the waters of El Masacre, that small international river crossable by foot. There in the sand is Hilarión's big footprint! So they'll get him on his way back. But, forever, the moon. That strange darkness. And a silence in which they can hear the nearby bees buzzing in the forest. Once again, the cattle passed safely before dawn. The cow left its hot dung-covered print on the Dominican side of the river. And disappeared as if it had been a shadow. Just like El Patú. Haiti calms his hunger now. The *bocó*! He does his work well.

Old pioneer Flores was dry, like the last cow's udder. From a wealthy native, Haiti had put him in the worst sort of misery. His gentlemanly boss's beard was now the beard of a beggar. He shows up beneath the old mango trees on the venerable hacienda where Sargent Tarragona had been milking cows since childhood. Now the old man watches afternoon die and disappear on the border like a distant bird. . . . Night comes. He remains beneath the old mango trees. Beneath the mangoes are two brilliant eyes, like fireflies, shooting hatred to the west, in the direction of Haiti. The corrals are empty. El Patú left his family hungry, without milk or vegetables, on the hacienda where the old man, noble and humanitarian, hid so many Haitians, to keep them from meeting their deaths on the morning of the Cutting.

Sleepily, the old man says: "After I saved them, I sent them off to Haiti, the country that begins at my property line. . . . But are they grateful . . . ? All they know how to do is steal . . . ! Without my cows I will die . . . ! Maybe Hilarión will return them! The Haitians won't let us live. . . . They have always been thieves, but now they are bigger thieves than ever. . . . Ah! That Patú! He's the one taking all the cows. Yesterday he took all the cows that belonged to my neighbor Mellizo. . . ."

And Patú kept taking cows. He left only their dung in the river, and the print of his unmistakable big foot. Patú was a sure guide on dark nights. He traveled better than the soldiers with their lanterns.

But one night the *bocó*'s hex failed to work. Chago Díaz took sure aim, because this time the moon favored the hunters.

It happened in Mellizo Feliz's corral, the old landowner from Santiago de la Cruz. The cornfield, its leaves tall and green, tricked Hilarión. Chago was waiting from the moment it began to get dark. Patú wasn't coming. But he would come! He didn't miss a single scent. The cattle stomped their feet, making a sound like yellow mangoes when they are about to fall. Dawn, with its cold needles, cut the hard flesh of Major Pedáneo who would kill the thief who stole his cows and nights of sleep. Patú showed up at last. Suspiciously he looked around. Like a leopard, he sniffed the breeze. He seemed to be making an effort to get the scent of Chago's body, hidden in the high corn. He sniffed and walked carefully. He stopped and proceeded again. He came back. Finally, he walked to the corral. Chago looked at him, black, very black, blacker than a raven. His teeth shone white, and he wanted to make himself as tall as the corral's mango tree. Chago Díaz took aim. He didn't miss. He shot at point-blank range.

The black man jumped very high. Was he trying to reach the moon? Chago would later say that he saw him leap higher than the mango tree, and thunderous phrases flew through the air, like parrots speaking Patois, the language of the Haitian farmer.

He called out to the *bocó* of Limbé, and fell heavily, like an enormous fruit from an infernal tree. On the dawn breeze, Patois screams lingered, pure animal speech, calling on the *bocó* to kill Chago. But Chago clings to the brown calf nearest him, so she will be the one who dies when the *bocó*'s curse takes effect. . . . Chago trembles beneath the full moon that is like an electric light, while Patú spews white foam from his red mouth. But Chago continues to embrace the calf, who is mooing sadly, because "the *bocó* will be here soon."

The shot woke the village, and neighbors began to arrive. The men went to Loma de Cabrera in search of the Captain, so he could identify the magic thief who lay dead in the cornfield. When they returned, Patú was long gone, and the brown calf continued to moo. The *bocó* woke up and tried to kill the calf because Chago had embraced it. The calf kicks as they squeeze the juice of a bitter orange on its lips and the farmhands pray beneath the moon's last glow. The calf cries again. And Patú is gone. The fence is broken because he knocked it down as he ran. Patú finally showed up on the banks of El Masacre, having almost crossed over. At that moment, all the cattle roared in fright. They were as nervous as the neighbors. Would Patú be back?

When the Sargent arrived, he looked toward the hills of Haiti and said: "We gotta burn those people like bad weed on a farm . . . ! The government should even order me to burn El Principe in Haiti's capital. We gotta rule Haiti so this damn situation done! Everything finished here . . . can't plant . . . can't live! Damn blacks take them all night long . . . ! And ain't even respect the women! Bad weeds . . . ! Gotta yank 'em out so they won't come back . . . !"

Haiti means hunger. Hunger knows no limits. Patú and his brothers will go on walking all night long. Night along La Línea is the only opportunity for Haiti to eat. A punished land: dry, rugged in the mountains. In the lowlands, lush with exotic countryside and complicit with the upper-class blacks who were schooled in Paris, like Hilarión's brother, known as Patú.

15

After Patú, many others like him stole cattle. The nights are rife with cattle, daggers, and screams. By day, the sun reveals a terrible loneliness, and men live in the fire of the breeze's eternal temperature that dyes them copper and reaffirms their ebony. Then there is silence, a crushing silence.

The black men continue stealing, which is to say satiating their hunger and assuming their martyrdom: they rob at night. They are like the *cocuyos*—a kind of tropical firefly—lighting up the night. Their eyes do not need lanterns or torches like the guards, who hunt them in vain.

THE COUNTRY BULLFIGHT CAME from Las Matas de Santa Cruz, where the thief nailed crosses in the hills. The landowners' rifles and everyone's dogs suffered the curse of the *bocó* from the Mole de San Nicolás.

They carved up the bull on Doña María's land. The black man is hesitant—strange tailor of the night—and neither his branding nor his carving is much good. At that hour, the soldiers approach El Masacre and Albert Loui opens the old cow or tar-colored calf. He disembowels it quickly, for his right to the animal is limited by how long the sun sleeps, while clouds cover the moon's traitorous eye.

Like a hunted man, from time to time Albert stops what he is doing and sniffs the breeze. And he thinks about the sons he left behind, hungry in Haiti. He doesn't know if they will kill him. The prisoners' daggers are sharp. Later, they decapitate the thieves and toss their heads across the river, to teach Haiti a lesson. Now that the sun is setting, Albert Loui works quickly. It is a cold night, but he doesn't feel it. He is cold. He is a dead man! Albert Loui knows this. He is working on the black calf he took from a farm at dawn. His sons will meet him at the river. Maybe he will get there alive . . . but no! He is already dead! Damned thoughts. Why does he think he is dead? He sniffs again.

Will they come . . . ? And, silent and imploring, he gazes out into the darkness of the vast savannah. *"Faim, faim!"* Hunger! Hunger!

The black men paid a high price for the meat. They paid with their black men's flesh. The *champetres*—Haitian rural police—will not allow the stolen cattle to enter their country. They punish the thieves with beatings, long lockups without a crust of bread. Sometimes they hang them in some far-off village where the *champetre*, who is mestizo, hates blacks, a bastard race according to Haiti's mixed bloods. In Haiti, there is hunger and racial hatred. The mestizos who study in Paris, or managed the great estates, look with loathing upon their brothers, the ebony race that lost its land and forever steals from Santo Domingo along the shores of El Masacre. Sometimes the *champetres* burn the thieves. The ash from the *champetres'* fires reveal mutilated toes. If Albert Loui gets to Haiti with his cattle alive, he might succumb to the *champetre*, his racial brother. Then the *champetre* will make deals with the Dominican owners, to return the cattle stolen by Albert Loui—just one more dead man. Albert Loui is dead already! That is why he doesn't feel the cold of the night on the immense savannah. He is decapitated now! He himself! Beside the tar-colored calf whose throat he has just cut. The daggers emerge from the bosom of the night. Like brilliant stars. Like hungry dogs. Suddenly. Albert will remain unburied until the sun, rain, and wind devour him. What will happen to Albert's small children? They still wait for him on the banks of El Masacre. Dawn will break, and Albert won't come home. Is he dead . . . ? They don't know. And there is no one they can ask. They will still be hiding among the reeds, like Haiti's mangy dogs.

16

Now the Captain orders them to bury the dead, although no one wants to obey his order. Or simply hide the bodies in some forest, far from the view of those walking by. These were the ruses of that "historic hygiene" that cleansed the foreign insect from the Dominican Republic's soil.

"We will bury them! It's better," said a soldier.

"You bury them if you like . . . ! Me: I'm not gonna dig a hole for no Haitian. Better my hands should bury a rotting rat. . . . But bury a Haitian man? I rather cut them off! Haitian man only good for stealing . . . ! Thieves you gotta cut their heads and leave 'em for other thieves. They dogs and swine. Or better to burn 'em, so they ain't stinking . . . !"

That was a tall soldier talking, a recruit named Angeles, a young man from La Línea, a native of the region of Santiago de la Cruz, whose grandfather, old Saint-Hilaire of French descent, had practically been made a beggar by the Haitian thieves. The strapping youth spoke, remembering sleepless nights when he guarded the fields and cattle. In those nights, a plague of black locusts finished off the yucca and corn. The thieves took everything.

Then, in the distance, the powerful bull could be heard bellowing; he was the favorite. He seemed to be announcing the robbers' approach. Sometimes that bellowing frightened the guinea fowl, and the fat pigs tied up beneath the orange trees. Everything had been taken. Even the last milk cows at the old man's house. The farmworkers would bring the tragic evidence each morning: the remains of beloved cattle, quartered and abandoned on the plain because, it seemed, daylight had surprised the thief and he was forced to leave his bounty behind.

The old man trembled, nervously smoking the old clay pipe he kept to remind him of better days. They had taken and slaughtered the big bull, a veritable family member. The whole family cried. Another day it was the cow, Carmelita. And the same story of thievery and abandonment on the savannah. The old man fell quiet, looking only in the direction of Haiti, and he wanted to burn all that damned land and all those men, who aren't even men because they're nothing but thieves! Grandfather Saint-Hilaire's blue eyes and Haiti's blue mountains in the distance. There was fire in the old man's eyes. And the next day, Grandfather Saint-Hilaire was dead. He must have died from losing Carmelita, the cow, on whose morning milk he had raised all his grandchildren.

All this consumed the mind of his grandson, the soldier Angeles, who refused to bury Haitians.

ON THE SAVANNAH, they begin to bury or burn blacks. Yusén, the black hotel owner, traveled in desperation from that place to his farm at Dajabón. He was married to Morgenia, the Dominican, who had given him a string of children who only spoke Patois. How was the man saved . . . ? "A true miracle," Yusén shrieked, bathed in blood, missing an ear and still bleeding:

"*Bon Dieu! Bon Dieu! Cela debacle! Debacle! Morgenia, vá Haiti, plont!*"

They told their story as they fled, taking what they could of their meager belongings. Ramoncito Donkey Eater's machete allowed them to escape the savannah. He was the prisoner they hated because he wouldn't lend them his horse before the Cutting. While Yusén is in the fields, burying his tribal brothers, burning most of them on orders from the soldiers, the prisoner they called Donkey Eater had also acquired another name: People Eater. Such was his capacity for killing. His machete's sharp blade rips through the air, attempting to behead Yusén. But Donkey Eater, or rather People Eater, is skilled. Yusén's right ear leaps from his head, because he manages to twist his body at the last minute. The blow, aimed at the head itself, lands slightly to one side, and instead of a head the savannah gains an ear, now lost among so many other severed members as Yusén leaps over pyramids of burning corpses. He avoids other sabers and clubs, although some of the blows impact his strong body. Still, he resists as he flees, arguing with the wind, and finally reaches Dajabón like an orphaned animal. His legacy will be the Cutting: the guillotine. Guillotine of plains and hills. Of night and day. Death sentence. With no possibility of appeal.

These were also Toussaint's and Dessalines's sentences. Juan Calvo's savannah butchery recalls that Haitian leader's phrase, aimed at the inhabitants of Santo Domingo: "I will hunt you like wild animals, all the way to the mountains." It is all part of this brutal sacrifice in which Yusén, the good black who had joined his blood with the black Dominican of Dajabón, escaped. Morgenia thought more blood flowed from Yusén that morning than there is water in El Masacre. She is desperate. The children are screaming. The neighborhood, that doesn't have a precise idea of what's going on in distant places, becomes alarmed. Yusén thinks: "The guards will be here any minute. They are coming to kill me. I must live." He goes into the courtyard. He takes some of his cow's droppings and fashions a plaster that stops the bleeding. He is missing an ear. But he sets about to save his life! Where can he go . . . ? To Haiti! He must cross El Masacre. . . . But he isn't thinking! It's been thirty years since he's left Haiti, and he doesn't know anyone there! He is Dominican . . . ! Okay, but he must get to Haiti, even if only to die. . . . The thing is, Haiti is his homeland. He must save his sons and his wife, Morgenia. Quickly, she has gathered pieces of clothing. Yusén can't think what to take with him to Haiti. His weakness makes him hesitate. He tries to decide.

What will he take . . . ? There is his goat . . . ! It's been two days since she's eaten, ever since he left. . . . The good, sad, cats. Michel, the dog, thin but gentle, sleepy. He mustn't leave them behind! Their hammocks, the children's cots, the cooking pots. Then he runs to the corral and catches the skinny mule—the only one he has—bought at auction. He will leave the children's young cows at Don Chepe's farm. He is a noble man, elderly now, once a general. Don Chepe will keep them safe. And maybe he can come back for them. Or maybe Captain Windbag will make off with them, take them to his estate at Mao. . . .

All of this goes through black Yusén's mind at the speed of light, with one ear missing and his cow dung plaster. Will the soldiers come . . . ? He must stay alive for Morgenia and his children. And they leave. They go to Haiti, which is to say to an unknown country. The poor family draws its first deep breath as it crosses El Masacre.

As he walks, now, on Haitian soil, Yusén Nataniel remembers Ramoncito People Eater. Not all Dominicans are like him! "The Dominicans are good!" And people said that Captain Windbag's grandfather was also a black from Haiti . . . ! So why did Captain Windbag, whose grandfather was also black, order the killing of all Haitian blacks . . . ? As he ponders this, he pushes the little mule he'd gotten a few days earlier at the auction in Alcaldía. It's his salvation. El Masacre is behind him, with that nervous mule's hoof prints embedded in its sands. At that moment, he remembers the story of Joseph and Mary on their burro, persecuted by the Romans. Behind were the thick *javillas*— luxuriant trees on the river banks. Yusén, beneath the sun, follows the yellow path that will take him to the town called Juana Méndez, where he doesn't know a soul. His life has been changed by a sentence handed down by an all-powerful man in my country. That man ordered: "All Haitians must die!" Like destroying a bunch of tin soldiers!

"WE ARE PUTTING one over on them!"

That is what Don David told me, the man whose job it was to distribute tracts of land, smiling contentedly with his toothless mouth from which a cigarette swings like a pendulum.

"Don't speak to me of humanity, nor of the weeds of the academy . . . ! We are putting one over on them! It's an old debt! A century ago these same blacks bled the Dominican people, beheading even inside the churches . . . ! We are cashing in!"

And he looked with hate at the green mountains, the blue mountains, the wrinkled mountains of Haiti.

In the late afternoon, already dressed in stars, the cries of a nearby pack of dogs could be heard.

"Listen to them . . . dogs. They are eating their masters. . . . It's the best they can do! To put an end to that shitload of Haitians once and for all."

From the small hill where we stood, I looked into the hazy distance. From one point ran the thin dogs, dry, with their long teeth, sharpened on their Haitian owner's endless fast. Two hungers: the dog's and the dog's owner who perhaps already lies dead on the Dominican savannah. Later, the dog will leave. But he will return to ford the river. He will visit the places where the killings took place. Something must remain. The dog is satisfied now, like Captain Windbag.

The thin dog comes and goes on its hunger march, just like the Haitians. Despite the horror of the night. Why does he return? To live. Or maybe to die! It's every night. Each night is a game of cards. If they kill the hungry man, who will know . . . ? Who will denounce them? In this vortex, the dead have no names. Not even numbers, like in a prison. If our mules trip over a corpse on the road, we will halt our mules and bury it. What man? For Don David, the dead man is not human. It was "a Haitian . . . only a Haitian. . . ." While we waited beneath the trees, Don David shifted his cigarette from one corner of his mouth to the other. He seemed sinister, in that bit of moonlight.

Before the ghostly man, at the moment when dusk closed in, I returned to my childhood emotions. Thin, strong, angular, slightly Asiatic in his features, loaded down with bullets and daggers, Don David reminded me of those frightening figures about whom my nanny whispered to me, so I would fall asleep. As evening descended upon that mountain, Don David seemed like a demon. A demon of the desert. And his sardonic laughter, the way he punctuated his stories of killing, died out in the night. As he finished each story, his voice evoked the sound of oars in deep dark water. At that moment, I had returned to the delirious time of my childhood, filled with spirits, elves, and other mysterious beings.

Meanwhile, the night felt suffocating—it suffocated everyone, especially me. Night was a void, painted black. Like Haiti's destiny. With Haiti's color.

17

Dajabón. The village was deserted. There was fear, a lack of news, and distress. A prudent discretion. No one wanted to talk. The Captain remained drunk. The Captain drank and drank and then drank again. At the tavern, every few moments he received messages, "information" from the different "services." Aside from details such as the number of victims, these messages enumerated the number of cattle recovered. He would laugh, then, drooling a brownish saliva, and his face would assume a ghostly color, like that of the corpses. When he laughed he looked like the Devil. He thought about his land in Mao. The pale-green grass. And his uncountable head of cattle, bounty of the maelstrom. The culmination of his proprietary dream. Drunk, he would talk about all that. He too had been poor. The Cutting had made him rich.

AT THE TAVERN, time dissolves. There is no limit on this earth, not for alcohol or death. Windbag is surrounded by acolytes who applaud his words and wit. Sometimes, when drunk, he's grabbed one of them by the scruff of the neck. No one protested. Other owners, men of a certain category, accompanied the Captain although they resented having to spend the night in that dive, among professional drunks, beneath the pale light of a kerosene lamp, because the town did not yet have electricity.

Who is afraid of Captain Windbag? Maybe he is thinking about an attack by armed Haitians. Windbag is a criminal and a coward. That's why he drinks so much. At the tavern, no one can leave his table. No one can smoke anything but Virginia tobacco either, because the Captain, who had been born in a shack, in a miserable neighborhood in Santo Domingo, couldn't stand the smell of any other tobacco.

The truth is, the Captain is a changed man. His chevrons had produced the miracle. Now he hopes to marry a beautiful young girl from Gazcue. His plans are brilliantly celebrated among the drunks. The Captain drinks as if he is toasting the God of the Cutting, the idol of the killing. An obese landowner, servile as a dog, drinks with him and trades scores for smiles. The Captain has his ways! They are drinking Barbancourt Five Stars. The Captain only drinks Five Stars, and he brings crates of it from the Haitian town of Juana Méndez, meaning he smuggles it in. There isn't a customs official who would dare question the Captain.

At night Don Lauterio is at the tavern. He is a merchant who is the middle man in the importation of Restauración coffee—the excellent bean whose price he multiplies by five, and whose growers have also died with the advent of the Cutting. Still, Don Lauterio smiles, his smile etched in brass like a carnival mask. He must protect his hide with the Captain! He must stay with him all night long, until he gets up to go, almost always early the following day. Don Lauterio thinks of his business, his scales rigged to deceive. It's business! But, now . . . ? Without blacks from Haiti . . . ! Will the berries rot in the hills . . . ? Will Restauración coffee be lost?

Don Lauterio, who claims schools aren't needed because his grandfather couldn't make an *O* and yet died rich, nonetheless thinks that Haitians are needed. But he doesn't speak, and continues to smile with docility, and the night unfolds with its grindingly slow pace, like that of a tortoise.

Dajabón's terrible loneliness. One can hear the wind howling in the leaves. The sound of glasses clinking. Alcoholic chatter, and the dense smell of those blond cigarettes from Virginia the Captain smokes. Sometimes the Captain nods off, and the others fall silent. He wakes suddenly when a lit cigarette burns out between his fingers.

Meanwhile, there is nothing but calm. No Haitians come seeking revenge. The only returnees will be dogs, beggars like their masters, who've taken refuge in El Cabo or Juana Méndez. The massacre continues, almost without permission from the pebbles in the river. The river that resounds in its waterfalls at La Garrapata and Loma de Cabrera, cautious like one more Haitian when it passes before the Dominican fortress. Is it afraid? Wordlessly, it makes its way to the Atlantic.

18

Anguish caused Don Sebusto's tobacco-colored lips to tremble. It produced a living tear in Francisco Seijas's only eye. Seijas owned an estate on the border, in Santiago de la Cruz. The Cutting—the massacre—knocked down the columns of that landowner's chapel.

When the Spanish conquistador came to the island of Santo Domingo, he walked the dry lands of Monte Cristy province, and, like all good Spaniards, built in two places that reminded him of the topography of his ancestral home on the peninsula: one was Partido and the other Santiago de la Cruz. Two little Spanish towns. They still resemble the beloved Spanish homeland. When one arrives in Partido or Santiago de la Cruz, one immediately thinks of Spain, despite the fact that one is right on the border and in imminent contact with Haiti.

The view stretches out until it exhausts itself over the vast savannah. That's what it must have been like for the Spaniard when his mules first trod that land at the time of the Conquest. From the lowlands, the traveler brings a tired spirit, depleted by the African heat of the valley surrounding Dajabón. The caliche road winds on and on, leaving Juan Calvo behind. As you go higher, it rises through small passes. As the gray disappears and a promising green begins, it seems as if the traveler will be able to see the stars more clearly. The breeze is like a silken caress, and the freshness of the heights finally appears. The route, a road constructed by the government, is bordered by haciendas on both sides. You can glimpse the houses through the branches of coconut palms.

The traveler has escaped the savannah's suffering.

White folks in that land of blacks. For years, troops coming and going during the revolutions that shook Santo Domingo passed through the small town. The old-timers kept themselves safe by paying off the officials with cattle that fed the urban fighters. These small-time bosses produced cattle and alcohol. It was the production of the Haitians who worked the sugarcane fields and the ranches. Francisco Seijas's other brother, Juanico, also lives in this town. He also produces rum and cows.

The two white farmers see what is happening, and they cannot understand it. There have been revolutions in the past, but the problem is enormous now. Everything seems paralyzed in Santiago de la Cruz, even the breeze in the pines. The story of these lives is the same as that of other farmers: they all own rustic, feudal, properties. Fields, cows, sugarcane plantations on the very border with Haiti. The cane is easily grown by the blacks. The process is finished off by thin horses and the mill, working beneath sun and moon. From the *guarapo*—the sugarcane's extract—they make alcohol. In this far-off place, Don Francisco doesn't pay taxes. It's easy to get around the law. The border is nearby, in his backyard. There are times when Don Francisco's cow grazes on Haiti's savannah.

His cows return at sunset. He is lucky. But at other times, they "don't appear." Because of the illegal commerce, silks and doubloons come through Don Francisco's courtyard that borders on the Republic of Haiti. He thinks: "Governments be damned! This is my house; this land belongs to me." And like any good Machiavellian, he offers food to the soldiers who pass his house, whether they are revolutionaries or government troops. It's all the same to him.

His philosophy is: stay on everyone's good side, especially those in charge. Dried out, of scant flesh, slightly hunched, with a long snout that resembles that of a rat, he hides his one bad eye behind dark glasses. Don Francisco is a bifurcated soul. Crafty, utilitarian, a good actor.

Those governments . . . so far away . . .

When he speaks, he looks at the corral and decides how many calves he will give the officials on their way to kill and be killed at Cerro de las Mercedes or any other of the nearby killing fields. The governments are far away: He knows how to buy immunity! The border is in his backyard, and there is no customs post there. No reason to count the hours these peons work! After the sun goes down, the embers in the mill oven turn Berenis Mandía's and Samuel Dass's faces red. The two men are longtime foremen, indifferent now to the dawn cold, as they keep watch over the molasses until it is ready to drink. That's how the cane, once in the field and waiting for the rains to let up, is transformed into alcohol. Then the product makes its way to Haiti.

Through this whole process, the earth has heard creole songs and Don Francisco's orders, also in creole.

At this time—Don Francisco's life is an example—the Dominican Republic cannot go beyond two tired words, "Dominican" and "Republic." No one knows about the place. Here, the only thing one hears is the pedestrian French of Haiti, and every day is the same as the one before. Day after day of crude production: more fruit—mangoes, avocados, planted by black hands—more calves and more goats, also raised by them for Don Francisco. And more blacks as well, children of Haitians who barely hear Spanish spoken.

Although there were robberies, he wasn't worried. Don Francisco knows he always wins because of the low salaries he pays his workers. When they told him a calf was missing, he shrieked so they would think he was angry. He knew all too well who the thief had been, and maybe even where the calf was . . . ! The thief might be Samuel, the guy who worked the oven, who worked quietly all night long and whose hands were missing some fingers swallowed by Don Francisco's mill. Samuel, who doesn't know the word "salary," who makes no demands, takes one of Don Francisco's calves! But Don Francisco needs Samuel.

The boss tells himself: "Better to lose a cow than a slave who is always ready to do my bidding...."

The Cutting has also passed by here, and Don Francisco saw everything and kept his mouth shut. Not a single protest. He knows it's against the law to protest in Santo Domingo. Not even the shrieks of Natalí, the oldest black man, who told of the Cutting, of the killings in his corrals. Natalí screamed like a hog at Easter. Don Francisco saw it all and kept quiet.

Like Natalí, all his workers were murdered. And Don Francisco continued tightlipped to preserve his good relations with the military "chiefs" who enjoy resting and drinking whiskey at his house. Whiskey served by his two beautiful daughters, deserving of trust. The two daughters share his goal: they would love to trap some officer of the Dominican Armed Forces. A captain! It doesn't matter if he's old or ugly. But a captain!

Old Seijas had cursed and criticized the "criminal" government. But when the patrol came to his house, he would speak ill of the Haitians. "We can't live! They steal everything! They're dogs...!" said quick-witted Don Francisco.

Then he repeated: "The best thing the government's done is kick 'em all out.... They're dogs! And bigger thieves than cats! They done me in! They done take all my animals.... This a great government! Long live the General...!"

That's how he mollifies the troops that pass: with hospitality and lies. The thug of a lieutenant, going by any name, later remembers the smile of one of Don Francisco's daughters. "That old man... he's a great man...! Great friend of the government...." (For her part, the girl is enchanted by the military man's ribbons.)

Don Francisco looks out, sees that the military visit has ended, and thinks he can talk now, to vent his anguish: "They can't bring silk anymore...! Even creole salt is bad, it comes from unsanitary mines and with more and more taxes...! I was used to all those things from Haiti... and now... damned government...! They should overthrow it! But where's the men in this country...? And we've got to go everywhere, to all the meetings called by the authorities of this new province, ain't good for nothing, and clap every time they say the General's name, and say yes to everything...! A working man can't live...!"

And now he looks at the plantations, burned by the summer fires. The scorching fires of La Línea. Who will plough the land? No one! It will go to seed...! And how will anyone live here...? He thinks about his girls. He hopes they will soon find a captain or lieutenant. It's the only solution.

"This is finished." The same words uttered by Rafael García, by Don Lauterio, and by Mistress Francina in Dajabón.

"I'll have to go.... I'll have to leave this land to the Devil!"

But at that moment the Captain's car drove up to his door. Don Francisco, like an actor, transformed himself. He burst into a macabre smile.

"Come in, Captain...! I've got a drink waiting for you here...!"

The Captain arrived drunk, staggering. He barely made it to the rocking chair. He began to snore right away.

Don Francisco said only: "Good man...! Such a good man!" And he looked at him as if he were an insect, disgusting and dangerous. Then he retired to the bedroom, grumbling in a low voice: "He should die! Are there no saints in heaven?"

And, with his one eye, he gazed through his window at the star-strewn sky.

19

Manuel Robert, Antolín, Ramoncito Donkey Eater, Chepe Lorenzo, and Loreto de la Cruz were all transformed. By the weight of the crime. Manuel especially. He had lost his mind. He had forgotten his skinny children, eaten by fever, gifts for El Masacre. He had forgotten his pregnant wife, Ramona. He had forgotten the "grave" on Juanico Rivas's dark land. He ran this way and that. A real Caligula of the savannah, employing all his weapons, all his energy, to destroy—his arms made for curing calves, for he was the best veterinarian in those parts. With his well-sharpened scalpel, he had performed difficult operations, without once losing his nerve. Now he has murdered old friends, whom he claims not to know. His eyes wander. He'd encouraged the troops with endless drink and crude phrases.

"Go on, compay Manuel . . . ! Clean these here cursed mountains once and for all. . . . And take your time, then you're going right into the *Guaidia* [the army] and maybe as Lieutenant . . . ! Boy, another drink . . . ! And long live the General . . . !"

Mad as he is, Manuel understands the promising offer. The army! Lieutenant, no less.... He imagines lieutenants make a lot of money.... Lieutenant! The charm works its magic: Lieutenant!

One told him: "Compay Manuel...don't weaken...! We Dominican and the General gonna help us.... You gonna be a lieutenant and I almost a captain.... We done with this sorrow...always bothering us."

One big circus, that savannah. That red savannah.

MEANWHILE, MANUEL'S CHILDREN, poor little ones, went hungry. "Where is *taíta*?" they asked. His wife sick, about to give birth; the cooking stoves unlit; the ancient grandmother talking to herself. And the roof thatch full of holes, barely able to keep out the water from the heavy downpours that soaked Dajabón at the time, after a year of drought. Poor Manuel Robert's house. He was a good man who only worked his land. Now he has become a drunken panther...! Why? Why does he do these things...? He doesn't know.

Manuel's brown shack looks like a dovecote compared with the Haitian Atis's house. Atis was able to flee to Haiti. Manuel's place, beneath the luxuriant *chachá* tree, is filled with neglect and hunger. Everyone looks at the savannah. They see nothing! He went that way, but *taíta* hasn't come back, he hasn't returned with the scant yucca of his fields to feed his naked ones! "Where is *taíta*...?" repeated the children, while their mother dozed. Dreaming of hunger and abandonment. And this is the Cutting.

BUT...THAT BLACK MAN...

Manuel seems to want to wake from his alcoholic haze. Is it Mandín, the Haitian boy who helped him with milking at the estate that belongs to Puzzo, the Italian master with his farm near the banks of the river...? Ah...yes...! But he's dead...! Who could have killed him...? And he stands there like an idiot, about to cry. Why does Manuel Robert want to cry now...?

And he takes off running, directionless. Where is he?

A boatload of gray dreams—the liquor—the worst there is, the stuff the soldiers bring from the Haitian merchant Theofil's storehouse.

Manuel trembles but then composes himself, because Corporal Encarnación Reyes encourages him. Why did that man talk to him like that? Why did he fear that man . . . ? He, Manuel, a bold man . . . !

But the truth is, the Corporal, with his pep talk, eggs him on.

"Ei . . . compay Manuel . . . ! Don't go weak on me now . . . !"

Then the alcoholic beast returns.

The other civilians, the so-called reservists, peasants involved in the crime, fight with Manuel. The things is, they want their names on the Captain's list. What do these men want?

"Even as just a beginner . . . I gotta get into the *Guaidia*!"

Corporal Reyes, who knows Manuel's history, tries to motivate him with other stories: "Remember, Manuel . . . this blackie killed your *taíta* . . . ! Left him naked! Your *pái* die like Jesus Christ, naked! By hand o' these blacks. . . ."

Manuel remembers. He is tired. He can't go on. It's the truth, but he can't go on. He is awake now. But who is he? He is another man. He is a product of the Cutting. Manuel doesn't know himself. And then he remembers the ranch, his children without bread, his pregnant wife. And he looks like a dead man.

OLD MAN ROBERT HAD come to the Dajabón plains like a leaf traveling on the whim of the breeze: a Sinbad of commercial opportunity, he traded the Virgin Islands seascape for the vast space of Dajabón's savannah. His life unfolded in a similar fashion to that of Mr. Broberg, the Dane. Instead of fish, cattle. He was lucky in his work. He started out as a servant at Fabbale's house, the man who sold silks and salt, at the same time as he speculated on cattle with buyers at Cibao and in the capital. Robert, the farmworker, saved his coins, those coins from Haiti, because in the village they didn't trade in Dominican money except on rare occasions, when some traveler came through. Days of hot sun and saving gouls—Haitian money—increased peoples' savings.

Finally, he bought a few head of cattle in Partido and sold them to interested parties. A lot of work, but a lot of savings too. After some years, he was able to emancipate himself.

Then he invested his savings in the rich promise of a farm at Doña María that painted itself green like the most magical and magnificent mosaic of cows and young beef bulls. Then came the cane fields, to take advantage of cheap black labor. Then the mill. With what he earned from the mill came the store, selling all manner of goods. And he became a powerful man, because back then it rained a lot and the grass was always green. He let his animals range free on communal land. He also had sons, and took them into his business. Eventually he died, leaving a noble and generous legacy. He was a gentle and charitable Englishman. But the same thing happened that always happens: his sons took it upon themselves to decimate his wealth, and only the land remained. And the thieves launched a war on that land that eventually left Robert's sons in misery.

The Robertses had traded good shoes for rustic sandals. From then on, Manuel worked as a farmhand. He also had his small field. From those times, Manuel remembers the planting songs, the *junta*, the *burricada*, and cooperative labor when friends help friends with half a day of work and for only a few sips of coffee. He remembered the couplets of the *toro montón* who, stolen by Haitians one night, strangled the boss the next morning; one of those anonymous sentimental romances that are heard at dusk from time to time while pasturing the cattle that belong to Puzzo the Italian along the banks of El Masacre.

But all this was yesterday. Now he walks around barefoot and with torn pants. He knows he cannot go to Guayubín, to the patron saint's fiesta, or buy from the canteen at the veiling ceremonies, peasant events in remembrance of the dead.

Yes, it was those damned Haitians who stole all the cattle.

NOW HE HEARD SCREAMS. And when Corporal Reyes reminded him of his father and his poverty, he changed horribly. He also heard promising phrases: The army.... Lieutenant! What's that...? It must be something big . . . ! But then he comes to his senses again. He thinks about his children. No, he is someone else now. He is no longer Manuel. Who is he?

Risking death, he deserted from his troop. He headed for Dajabón. It was enough already, even if he never got to be a lieutenant. That one, that's the house! It's shut up tight! Has the woman died . . . ? And the children . . . ? He is awake now! The sun is strong. Once again, he is Manuel Robert.

When he gets to his house, his sons who once leapt to embrace him when he got in from the fields, flee . . . ! They cry out in desperation. What do his children see . . . ? Why do they cry out . . . ? It's *taíta* . . . good *taíta*. . . .

But his sons keep on running and shouting. They avoid him. They do not allow him to kiss them. Manuel almost cries. Why don't his children love him?

The children flee. The children scream. It wasn't Manuel! It was another man they saw. The children tremble before the caricature of the crime . . . !

He lay down by the courtyard tree. And he too began to cry. And this is the Cutting.

20

During this blood storm, the men in the villages who profited from the land and from their new slaves raise their voices in protest. Dajabón's shacks heard timid laments. Were they protesting *against the crime* or against a violent change to a way of life, to a system of production, that had sustained the laziness of the frontier Dominican . . . ?

This is something I've thought about over the years, and I think about it again as the savannah burns. Landscape of smoke, men and farms in flames. Everything had to burn! That was the command. Even the men, as in the burning of heretics among white Europeans in the sixteenth century! This another auto-da-fé.

For seven days, the field dog ate his fill, its spirit so dry it seemed to float on the wind, like the *chachá* leaf. A dog, as much at home in the hills as on the savannah, whose destiny it was to be born so he could die. Of hunger. Not unlike the Haitian black man. And that's why the dog too knew all the shortcuts and hidden routes. In one leap, like the Haitian, it crosses the river and attacks Joussard's and Doña María's cows. And it runs the length of the small river, dodging the bullets fired by the landowners' rifles. Dry soul, vagabond, part of the landscape, guided by scent, it sniffs the stones, devours the distances. Border dog, Haitian dog. In life and destiny. Stealing so as to be able to eat. And in the end, dying tragically. The Dominican peons use their machetes to kill the dogs that eat their calves. These peons use the same weapons to kill the thieving Haitians. And once dog or man is dead, they are buried in silence, disappearing like stones tossed into the river's depths.

I am writing now by the light of the stars. The village is but one more among the dead. From Chacuey, along the river, where there are some petroglyphs etched thousands of years ago by other men attacked by the spears of Spanish conquerors, comes a cold night wind carrying the message of Chacuey's dogs. Distant dogs. But why do I feel them so close to my house, in the middle of the night? Their barking, more than laments, more than fiesta racket, suggest protest to me.

21

The ditch was dug with big tractors, sent by the government. Long and straight, like a great wound across the plain's breast, the plain that has always swallowed men and upon whose earth, fertilized by corpses, the grass will be greener now. The cattle graze there, on land that is open and unrestricted, adorned by the mango trees planted by those who walked it. The ditch is huge: a great mouth devouring Haiti.

Why is the sky so sad . . . ? It seems as if the afternoon wants to water the strange seeds, a crop of men.

The troop came, silent. Now they were ditch diggers. The men brought something besides the exhaustion of their journey. They also suffered from the listlessness and depression caused by drinking beneath a hot sun.

The prisoners were in the lead, victims and victimizers. Their disgrace, their misery, prison luck, had launched them one day to La Línea.

"Yes, compay . . . I came to the border to do me five year. . . . But happen I couldn't stand it. . . . Don Crescencio done fence all the land. He push us out. My máma tell me: 'There's no more wood, go get some wood . . .' and out looking for dry branches, that's when Don Crescencio come: 'Get away from that, thief . . . !' We couldn't work. All belong to Don Crescencio. Fence and all! Couldn't even find a crab in the river . . . he fence that too! But one day I crawl under the wire and go fishing. All happy 'cause I got me four fish. You know they raise cattle there, but no meat for us . . . they send it to the capital . . . ! And a bottle of milk, they don't sell it to us, even for the children. . . . Then they tell me Don Crescencio take my old woman prisoner 'cause she got on his farm and was weeding a field . . . keep from dying of hunger . . . ! And I say, 'This is finish here!' And I go kill Don Crescencio. . . ."

"Just like that happen to me. . . . I kill the surveyor . . . guy went on my *taíta*'s land to measure for the company. . . . Say the land ain't belong to *taíta* . . . even we all born there. . . ."

"But look here . . . I never has killed a cat before. . . . I come here 'cause over Villa Vasque the land bad for watering . . . and I wanna make a farm, in them abandon hills, 'cause over there all belong to the rich and I tired of working day after day . . . and I working when the *Guaidia* grab me go kill farmers. . . . I no good now."

"But look, don't you worry. After this, we go to the *Guaidia* . . . big boss. What I like is the *Guaidia*. Working right away . . . I no more gonna be a leech, cleaning canals for nothing . . . and nights the mosquito biting. . . . Don't you worry . . . us reservists we going up. Skinny and tired, but going up. . . . If the hunger and this damn firewater don't kill us, maybe we get there. . . . Stay strong . . . ! This gotta end. . . ."

These reservists return to the village drunk and tired. They suffer from fevers and strange maladies. Some will die from unknown diseases. Others, like private Patricio, will go crazy. After the Cutting, many madmen roamed the village. Almost everyone's nerves were destroyed. There would be obsessives who couldn't sleep at night. And they all asked themselves the same terrible question: Why had they killed?

They'd barely eaten a bit of bread when they robbed some miserable shop in that lonely place. Sometimes they'd find rotten cod in the store, and dry bread, dry as the pebbles in the ditch, food for rats. But, of course, there was always rum. The stores in our countryside always have alcohol.

Manuel Robert, his eyes gray and red, appears like someone silently shouldering a large and heavy cross, without complaint, close to madness. Sometimes he feels words dying in his throat. His body, strong like a mahogany tree the morning they captured him, is broken now. He thinks of his children. Why do his children flee from him? This is his permanent question.

His face is the color of ash. He is no longer a powerful man. He seems ancient. Seven nights of crime and atonement have taken their toll. His face has settled into a web of premature wrinkles. And his children . . . ? That's the question that pierces his heart and fractures his small peasant brain. The one he left with a fever died. Did they bury him? And who will pay for the loss of his child . . . ? His wife is on her deathbed; neither she nor the children have tasted food since they've been unable to go to the fields, fearful of being taken for Haitians and murdered by the troops of prisoners.

He passed in front of the store at the edge of the village, and some of those standing in the doorway were shocked to see him: "So long . . . ? So long . . . ? Is that Manuel Robert . . . ? Man . . . ! All hunch over and his face like death. . . . Was such a strong man . . . !"

When they arrived at the Dajabón fort, the Captain who discharged the soldiers was there. The reservists received orders to go and change their clothes. They would abandon their dirty rags and put on the vile uniform of common criminals.

"Go on, dress yourself like tigers . . . !"* roared the Corporal on duty.

Manuel Robert had a violent awakening when the Sargent of the Guard gave him those degrading clothes, the garments of my country's thieves or criminals—or sometimes its politicians. He, Manuel, who had obeyed the commands of the General who ordered him to

---

* "Tiger" is a very Dominican term with a lot of embedded meaning. Dominican men often refer to themselves as tigers, a designation with macho implications.

behead: making him a prisoner . . . ? Was it a mistake . . . ? Didn't they mean someone else . . . ?

But the Sargent insisted. The same who on the savannah had urged him to kill more men. The same little Sargent who had whispered that he, Manuel Robert, would be a lieutenant in the army. . . .

There was a situation at the fort. It was caused by a "reservist" who had resisted becoming a prisoner. It was an order. An order from the General in the capital. An order the Captain had to carry out, afraid that he would be forced to don the same uniform. An order! And orders are to be followed!

The thing is, the General is an able politician. Politicians change colors like salamanders, according to their interests, their "success." The word "success," in my country's politics, is self-explanatory: success without shame, without worrying about how you got there.

MANUEL AND HIS COMRADES appeared before a nervous judge, thin like a scrawny bird. The judge asked and asked again. He demanded they tell him their stories. No one responded. Then the judge dictated a sham history to a skinny sickly secretary in a state of permanent drunkenness.

Manuel and his comrades don't speak. They ask themselves what is happening. They understand nothing.

The gaunt judge continues dictating. It's a colorful story. He dictates again. He keeps going. After a while, he is worn out and sends to the storehouse for more rum. They take Manuel and his comrades to the fort. Outside the dictation can still be heard. The judge continues to speak. . . . The judge is dictating Manuel's "declaration."

22

After the Cutting, the prisoners have become Captain Windbag's mule drivers. The cattle must be counted and sent to his far-off estates.

"Uooo ... Uoooo ..."

"Cow ... Uooooo ... !"

"Damn animal, git!"

"Eh ... compay ... close that gate. The cattle gitting out!"

"Damn cow ... git in ... ! Uoooo!"

"Git on in here, Candelón, git in!"

"Uoo ... Uoo!"

Energetic call of the mule driver, the shepherd, that at times has a mystic lilt, almost religious at dusk.

Aniceto de la Cruz. A king of cattle. The best shepherd of them all. Great rider and great herdsman. He always does it right, although now, as a prisoner, the Captain pays him nothing. A prisoner, in this place, is a slave. Aniceto knows this, and says sadly: "A prisoner ... is almost the same as a Haitian."

And he continues: "Uoo ... ! Uoo ... !"

The cattle seem to understand Aniceto's commands. Commands in Spanish. But from time to time Aniceto sings to the cattle in Patois: *"Allé ... allé. ... Esperens. ... Allé, vache. ..."*

"Damn cow ... she must be remembering her old black owner, Fran Luí. ... Look at her. ... Look at her ... she wants to cry. ..."

"Allé ... vacá ... uoo!"

"Compay Tatán ... Compay Tatán ... I'm lost ... that cow givin' me the evil eye. ... Yes, since I kill the mailman from Restauración. Poor old man. He my friend. And since then I cursed."

Aniceto breaks off his monologue.

Then once again, his energetic voice: *"Vacá ...!* Uoo! Devil of a cow. ..."

"Ay ... Tatán, git over there ... uoo. ... Careful! Don't let this cow run off to Haiti ... Tatán. ... This cow belongs to the government ... and if you lose one, you pays with you skin."

"Uooo! Grab that! Rope that one! Look at 'em jump. Look like its owner taught this young'un to dance the *luá.* ..."*

He barely breathes between shouts and commands.

"Goodbye. ... See? They paying attention to you and giving me the evil eye! Even the cow ...! Yeah, this one belong to the old man in Restauración!"

"Careful, compay, careful ... these cows been counted ... and the Captain coming today to see his cattle. ..."

Aniceto de la Cruz, erect, agile on his mule. He seemed sad remembering his crime. "Even the cow giving me the evil eye," he said. He remembered everything then, in spite of the shouts and bellowing cattle, in the midst of a cloud of dust that stank of cattle shit and piss.

Aniceto's crime was one of many caused by hunger this relentless summer. Drought. Drought along La Línea. That dawn, so long ago now, he couldn't put up with it any longer. His wife was pregnant, because along the border, women have lots of children, just like pigs. And his parcel, Aniceto said, "was like a mangy dog." He had cried to

---

* A reference to the Haitian vodú god Lwa.

the heavens. And the heavens didn't respond. His favorite saint failed to bring the miracle of rain. To make things worse, the night before the Haitians had stolen his favorite cow. His wife was dying. In this far-off land there are no public clinics for the peasants. She had the fever already. And his land had cried forlornly from lack of rain. He walked out of his shack. All he could see was the bad grass they called *Madame Michel* and that other bad grass, resistant to the sun, they call foxtail. . . .

And he'd killed the mailman coming down the road, an old man who sometimes ate at his farmhouse. He didn't know how it had happened. The mailman lay beneath the stones of the mango grove that stretched to Restauración. And his wife died too, because there was no help for her, and they'd taken him prisoner to Monte Cristy. The mailman was only carrying papers and hadn't understood anything because he didn't know how to read. . . . What did he use to kill the mailman? A dry stake. And now what . . . ? Yes, maybe Sambá the Haitian can save him . . . ! Should he run . . . ? But no . . . ! And his wife . . . ?

Before he fell prisoner, Sambá the old Haitian fortuneteller had come by. He was his neighbor, and he told him he would never sleep again, that they would take him prisoner. . . . He didn't run. He was crazed but still thinking about his wife. She could no longer talk. And his small children would die when they took him to prison. When the guard came to get him, he was crazy as a loon.

"Ah! If it would only rain! Ah! Ah! If only the yucca plants hadn't gone to seed. . . . Ah! If it would rain!"

He continued babbling.

"Ah! If it would rain. . . ."

And when the men pushed him on ahead, he could only repeat: "Ah . . . ! If it would rain. . . ."

POOR ANICETO DE LA CRUZ, dressed in blue, in the suit the government sent for the prisoners. The anonymous mail carrier sleeps by the side of the road that goes to Restauración, among the pines beneath hard gray stones.

"Uoo! Uoo!"

The corral couldn't hold any more cattle. But more cattle arrived. The prisoners, under threat of death, hadn't lost a single one. A cow is worth more than a prisoner. And the Captain wants them all!

Aniceto was going through the corral. He attended to some wounded animals. Someone had told him he would win his freedom getting the cattle ready for the day the Captain would come.

That's why he was singing today, joyous at times, sad at others. Meanwhile, he cast his eyes over valleys and hills and spotted those specks—brown and black and red, of every color—cattle that had to be driven to the village of Loma de Cabrera. The cattle ran, urged on by men dressed in blue—the prisoners—who were driving them. They had sullen faces. Some were thinking about their distant lands, from where they'd emigrated by way of crime and prison. They sang typical roundup songs, sentimental songs like the beads in a peasant rosary. The cattle ran and behind them the shepherds, almost all of them on foot except for a few who were riding lame mules or broken-down horses. They were closer to the specks now, and could see the color of that calf and that old bull's wrinkled horns.

The Captain and Major are coming today! We've got to round up all the cattle!

"COMPAY MIGUEL, is it true what they saying . . . ? The General send every prisoner and every reservist a couple good milk cows and a young beef bull for ploughing . . . ? If it true, we saved . . . ! Look . . . ! I in love with them two calves. . . ."

"Well, that what they say . . . ! And if they give us the Haitian's farms and two little animals, we gonna be happy. . . . I gonna bring my woman over, she alone in Jánico since I stole that piece of cloth. . . . For one piece of cloth I take in the night I got more trouble than Christ. But listen, Simplicio . . . I believe it when I see it . . . I don't think . . ."

The specks kept on walking over the mountain's green shoulder. They looked like toy cows on a green cloth, a child's presentation. The specks flowed over the mountain's spine and descended like an avalanche onto the brown plain. Meanwhile, the breeze carried sweet songs and vulgar words.

"Pancho . . . Pancho . . . Cleto . . . ! That's a shortcut . . . a shortcut . . . ! If you go that way, you end up in Haiti . . . ! And this calf know its owner miles away. . . . Remember yesterday, that brown cow. . . . Watch where they going! Pancho, you know one of them bull worth two of us . . . ! They belong to the government . . . ! If we lose one, they cut out your tongue . . . !"

They call the second in command, the foreman Juan Zenón, Juanico Dead Cow. He knows the story of the cow one of the prisoners had to chase all day until it disappeared over the border into Haiti. Where is that prisoner?

He fled to Haiti, or he is buried beneath the avocado tree by the side of the road. His comrades, who drive the cattle, will faithfully obey the Captain's orders: lost cattle, hanged prisoner.

In the huge corral, too small now, the cattle are frightened, and the air deafened by voices, bellowings, kickings, gorings, and harsh orders.

Suddenly a strong wind surges. It clouds everyone's eyes. No one can see. The sun hides, and branches fly through the air. The hot savannah's earth flies on the wings of the breeze like a simoom in the desert. The men feel as if they are choking. The cattle too. The cattle break free of their fetters. They run in all directions. In the tornado, hooves destroy animals, men, and horses. The hooves cut like knives. The infernal spectacle has upset the village, toward which the wild avalanche of cattle advances. They uproot crops, trample men, and flatten houses. Where is the Captain? He hasn't yet arrived. This saves him. After the dust settles, some men continue to run. They are prisoners trying to round up the cattle that didn't manage to get to Haiti. Aniceto is on the ground. He is barely able to speak. Blood flows from his ears and mouth. Hundreds of cows have run over him. He half tries to struggle to his feet, in order to carry out the Captain's horrendous orders, the Captain who owns all those cattle that in great part have gone to Haiti. But he cannot get up. Aniceto is going to die.

"Those cattle are counted . . . ! And the Captain's coming today, . . ." he says from where he lies in the sand. . . . Go get 'em . . . !"

He only managed to spit out those words, his mouth in the sand, as he died in the arms of some prisoners, covered with earth and cattle shit. One of them, looking at him, said: "The mailman . . . the mailman. . . . God's punishment . . . !"

When they pick him out of the sand, the foreman Juanico Dead Cow, devoid of tenderness, says only: "Ave María Jesús . . . ! The cows' hooves cut like saws . . . !"

Aniceto is just one more. No one will remember him. This is La Línea. But there is more to come. Soon the Captain and the Major will arrive. The prisoners wait, perhaps for death. Who will be held accountable for the cattle that fled to Haiti? Who will answer to the Captain for his cows?

The prisoners have a single thought: what just happened isn't about decent people. It is a curse from Haiti.

23

The Captain and the Major arrived. They issued their orders in rapid succession. The cattle to their estates, in Mao, and Aniceto to the cemetery. He's a prisoner. A prisoner is worth nothing. A heifer is more valuable.

After their automobile disappeared in a cloud of the highway's yellow dust, the specks of cattle followed, lumbering along to the beat of the mule drivers' songs. Like Aniceto, they too were prisoners. The cattle disappeared in the distance. And the songs could no longer be heard. The prisoners' hopes disappeared with them. The road had swallowed the Captain and the Major. The cattle too.

"JUAN DE DIOS . . . ! How I dream about that pregnant *joquita*, and I care for her too . . . and all for nothing . . . for nothing! . . . Just so no one rat on you. . . ."

"*Asina memo, Baitolo . . . ! Ná noj ha valío bregai.* . . . And they telling the General done say them cattle was for the prisoner and the *reseivita*."

The eyes of Juan de Dios, the man who speaks, fly like birds across the peaceful landscape. His gaze follows the long route wounded by thousands of hooves. Hooves that beheaded Aniceto de la Cruz.

He loved his *joquita* and *berrenda* as if they were two women, and the Captain made off with them. For the Captain, they were just two more cows. He didn't know them, because the rich don't have to know their cows, only how many they own. Just as they do not know the suns or moons. Those are for the peons to know, and they are prisoners now. The prisoners live out their years of captivity in the stables that belong to the captains, while crosses multiply across the land. Useless law speaks of such punishments as "public works" and "containment."

But for Juan de Dios the young calves were lucky charms. He thought his calves would bring him luck. And now they were taking them off to slaughter. They were driving them to the fields of Mao, to sell them later to the highest bidder. And he had loved them so . . . !

He is sad, in his blue prisoner's uniform. At Loma de Cabrera, the prisoners wear coarse blue sackcloth. In the lowlands, in Monte Cristy and Dajabón, they wear stripes, as denigrating as the prison itself. Juan de Dios wears blue. The Cutting at La Vega sent him to prison for stealing cattle, and then the government sent him to La Línea to murder men.

Like Juan, everyone was stunned. Their souls had disappeared with the cattle. La Línea: cattle, trees, prisoners, blood. There are no more Haitians. But there is a dull ache in each Juan de Dios who has nothing left but regret. Not even a single calf!

"If I'd known this game, I would have got mine. . . . I'd have made a run for my house in the confusion . . . ! I thinking I getting rich, and now everything filth and blood and cover in cow shit; all for the Captain. . . ."

"Shut up, Perico . . . it gonna be okay! Wait . . . I know how to write. . . . I got a plan. The schoolteacher tell me. . . . Sending letter to the capital, so the General know what's going on . . . !"

"Good idea . . . ! I was getting all hot and bother! That fucking Captain just up and took off with all the cattle . . . ! Fool . . . ! He don't know what tomorrow bring. . . ."

"Victoriano, friend, I bothered by this thing. I was thinking of bringing my woman, raising a family. . . ."

"But we ain't lost everything yet. . . . We gotta do away with that Captain. . . . He gonna get his, like sin itself. . . . That shark's fins can't cut wood. *Se fuma ei túbano* and that calf gone . . . ! And shit for us. . . . Prisoners we ain't made of nothing. . . . Me, Rupeito Cigarán, I ain't gonna drown in a trough of water. . . ."

THE CONVERSATIONS CONTINUED, bathed in pain. It was the response to so much hope of ownership, dashed once and for all by the Captain's order. And orders are to be obeyed. The cattle for him. The dead, like Aniceto, whose name he didn't know, to the cemetery. And the other prisoners to the barracks.

Days later, a letter arrived in the capital, and the investigation commenced. Captain Windbag roared with rage. The prisoners were lined up, beneath the ten o'clock sun, and the Captain passed from east to west with the threat on his lips. The death sentence was easy enough, although Congress had struck it from the books. Who cares . . . ? A prisoner is worth less than a calf. Almost as much as a Haitian. . . .

The Captain's face showed signs of terror. He was waiting for the military investigation and had anticipated it. He paid one hundred pesos to anyone willing to be an informer. All the cattle were gone, and all hands empty. Cattle are charms. But money not so much Victoriano, Perico, Juan de Dios, and all the rest wanted nothing more than the return of their beloved cows . . . *joquita . . . berrenda . . . the little darkie . . . the torete motón*. . . . The troop refused to talk. The letter, scrawled in poor grammar on butcher paper, would mean the guillotine for Captain Windbag.

The military council arrived. An anonymous letter, signed only "the prisoners," was the death sentence for that Caligula of the plains, who smoked Virginia tobacco and drank Barbancourt Five Stars.

The Captain had tried to corner the cattle as he had cornered alcohol. The great herd did the Captain in, like the hoof that had pierced

Aniceto's breast, planted now like an anonymous mango tree in the black earth of a ranch at the edge of the village.

The council dictated its findings, and Captain Windbag was expelled from the army's ranks.

The Captain is destined to wander from now on, docile, humble, unknown, beneath the great oaks of the plazas in the nation's capital. Who knows him these days? Almost no one!

The Major came to a similar end. He fell like Aniceto beneath the cattle's hooves.

SPRING SMILES. EVERY ABANDONED estate is paradise for the hunger of those who, like Juan de Sena, only knew how to kill and beat resonant drums. The parcels of land, with their fruit trees, are as alluring as young girls. The landscape is populated now by whores, songs, daggers, and farms. Meanwhile, the banana trees are heavy with fruit sowed by Haiti.

Now the prisoners' hope lies in a piece of land, land for those who never owned it. Serfdom, with only a scant right to food. The coffee growers' stepchildren or eternal fieldworkers for the large landowners on plantations as big and wide as the sky. So much land and so much sky, but without saints, worked by the wretched, where there wasn't even a tiny field for their children to play. There were only two paths there: slavery or crime pushing you to La Línea. Difficult to be a man. Simple slaves. Slaves in the faraway provinces. Slaves, once more, on the border.

24

The judges arrived, among them the one who'd interrogated Manuel Robert.

These judges were thin, languid men, and tormented. More than judges, they were liars. Their job was to distort the events. Some had a yellow cast and suffered from deep melancholy. These newcomers to the village appeared to be suffering. They had been created for, and were destined to carry out, a special law. Before leaving for the border, they'd received their instructions: they would attribute outrageous relationships to the miserable reservists and peasants who had carried out the massacre. A government minister, in the capital, had devised the strategy, designed to reflect a process of personal antagonism between Dominican farmers and shepherds and black Haitians.

In my notebook, written back then, I read these notes:

Today three judges arrived to try the peasants who slit peoples' throats on orders from above. A new judiciary has created a new law. According to Mistress Francina, the three judges showed up at the inn. One of them is an old guy, thin and sickly, who coughs incessantly. Another, an older man, has a nervous tic that causes him to move his head all the time, from side to side, as if saying no. The third is a drunk. When they arrived in town, the first thing one of them asked was where are the whore houses and if there were a lot of easy girls. Poor judge. In this village, there isn't even electricity. There is solitude but no light. Prostitutes don't come to this desert. In the gambling dens, there are only armed men who tell interminable stories of killing.

The judges quickly embarked upon their mission. The comedy was carried out with all the trappings of justice, and they didn't even have the decency to remove the statue of Christ from the inquisitor's desk. But the judges ended up crazed. The accused answered their questions honestly: they had killed on orders from the Captain. Then the judge made up a story and dictated it to the stenographer. And so the annals of our jurisprudence were padded with lies.

In that comedic and cruel manner, they satisfied the Haiti of diplomats, the Haiti of commercial transactions, the Haiti of mulattos educated in Paris who would trade the blood of their brothers for a few coins offered them by the strongman who rules my country.

Haitian politicians made a great deal from the incident: a whole new harvest. The very Haitian politicians who charge the sugar mills fifteen pesos a head for every Haitian laborer working in the Dominican Republic's harvest lent themselves to this other, horrendous, harvest. And thus "indemnification" to the victims, with which they built their mansions in residential neighborhoods. Meanwhile, the thousands of maimed wandered Haiti's deteriorated lands, stealing the very fruit they planted in the Dominican Republic. Dying little by little.

TO THOSE PURPOSES THE sad make-believe judges worked hard, dictating their fables. There is no difference between these judges and the reservists they accused. They all obey the orders of the man in charge. It's the judges' turn now.

Photographers followed after the judges. They took pictures of the reservists, dressed as prisoners, inside Monte Cristy's fortified walls.

These judges disgusted me, and I refused to have anything to do with them. Did they seem like pigs to me? They ate the bread of blame.... But... wasn't I too a pig? That's how my conscience recriminated me. Nevertheless, I say: No, I am not! I am taking notes on the crime! I'm here to denounce it! If I kept silent, I would be the same as the judges, who arrive at the inn each day, emaciated, to consume a plate of lentils, and will forever remain silent.

"A lot of work, huh ... ?" I ask one of them, ironically.

The poor guy doesn't get my irony, and responds: "Yes, we are very busy ... it's a lot of work ... !"

I look at him and think about my country's drama and my own. Like me, these judges were forced to this land by misery. Life lends a helping hand to the university graduate without a future. Sometimes he reaches old age, as in the case of this judge, who speaks tenderly of his wife and children back in San Carlos. He sends his entire salary home, and it barely satisfies the needs of such a large family. A young academic also accepts these judicial scraps out of need, like a dog swallows a piece of meat even though it is poisoned.

These men accept this job this caricature of a job—because of the small and great tragedies of the Dominican situation. Their work is recorded by photographers who take pictures of the "delinquents." The judges have almost finished, because they were instructed to wrap it up in a month's time. They had to interrogate thousands of peasants. In their imaginations, they invented struggles, great battles between bands of invading Haitian peasants and bands of Dominicans. Now the resources destined to the farce were exhausted. That morning the photographers would come. They were the real judges of the great comedy.

The poor lawyers, who served as magistrates overseeing the judges, were reduced to the same level as the reservists: two types of victims of misery in my country. There was one difference, though: the reservists were unschooled. They didn't know the weight of the cross they bore. For the hungry university graduates, the circumstances were even more cruel. They knew the crime they were committing. In resignation, they let themselves be photographed with the accused. Accused by their conscience! As they focused their cameras, the photographers seemed to be laughing at these judges. But if you looked long and hard at their faces, you would see signs of martyrdom. The judges . . . the reservists' comrades. A true portrait of our national misfortune.

The judges' drama should be told in all its horror. In my diary, there are three notes, written early one morning while the village slept:

A few moments ago, Rosón, the most downtrodden of these poor lying judges, hanged himself from a rope in my bedroom. In the modest house, where we sleep on small soldiers' cots, I suddenly felt something grabbing at my mosquito netting. I couldn't see that well in the dark. I felt the house that lodges the inn overcome by emotion. I turned on the light and was astonished to find a man hanging from a rope he had just rigged! I quickly cut him down, with a machete I keep beneath my bed. When I cut the noose, the man fell. Because of his long legs, his neck hadn't broken. When he fell, I saw it was Rosón, the judge. His face was covered in tears. Crying, he implored: "No . . . ! no . . . ! . . . I cannot live. . . ." (Surely the man is crazy.) I called the doctor. He came staggering in, drunk. The distraught judge kept on crying: "I must die . . . ! I must die . . . !" The man's agitation obliged us to tie him down, as day dawned. This is the longest night! Dawn hasn't come yet.

They brought the other judge from the tavern in the middle of the night, in a state of alcoholic prostration. Poor judges! Only one of them made it through. One day he came to see me secretly and said: "I'm going . . . enough already, enough!"

And he left. Later I learned that the regime's police had beaten him and put him in jail. Where is he?

But there are other judges, those of the first order. These too have begun their work. They hear the accusations against the "murderers," according to their crimes, and automatically condemn them. The judges gather voluminous files of papers. In another village another judge, downcast and dry, who looked like an old cow, carried out his "duties." He passed sentence after sentence. Like the Captain, who drank and drank.

25

The judge had acted with record speed, in line with the orders he had received. The day came when all the trials were finished. And the judge got ready for his ascension in the judiciary. The judge was hopeful, just as the reservists had been. The latter expected to be given small farms and a few cows.

My government informed Haiti, and above all Washington, that "the criminals responsible for the border events had been sentenced by the appropriate Court of Law."

Two tragedies ended then, and others began: those of the reservists and those of the presiding judges.

The judges went home, stripped of their provisional powers. Magistrates without extra restitution except four months' salary earned in the blinding sun of that remote place. They would live forever in the photographs. But . . . is Haiti satisfied?

The reservists also returned to their far-off shacks. One afternoon a rumor of bugles and military doings reached the cells. It was the General himself, who would be coming to Monte Cristy.

Loreto de la Cruz had never seen him. He had heard people speak about him as about an extraordinary being. What would the General be like . . . ? Loreto wondered. He must be like those evil Haitians in our children's imaginations: a boogeyman, the Haitian who eats children. Such is Loreto's infantile imagination. He is childlike, in spite of his muscles and bull-like strength.

Chepe Lorenzo imagines him very tall, like the trees on his land, trees that had given shade along the road to all the revolutions. That's what the General must be like.

A few had seen his likeness in an out-of-focus picture in some old newspaper. But they couldn't really remember.

The sergeant on duty opened the prisons and ordered the men out. They lined them up. In front was El Morro—a nearby monument by the sea. You could see the white sand of the prison courtyard and the khaki of military uniforms.

Finally, the General appeared. He was wearing all his medals. The sun shone on the gold, silver, bronze. A blue suit, an erect man topped by a gray head that nevertheless appeared young.

"As you have fought for the country," he told them, "that my government defends, I have come to reward you. . . . You are free! You may go home! I advise prudence, order. The authorities will not bother you in any way. You are patriots, and the government appreciates your condition as reservists!"

Then he walked up and down the lines of prisoners. The General shook each man's hand. His own hand was delicate, slender, refined. In each hand, he placed ten pesos. A bribe.

Loreto de la Cruz stared at him and Manuel Robert too.

"And he's . . . the General?"

"I can't believe . . . !"

They thought he would be bigger, stronger, larger than life. Aren't generals tall men, like the mahogany trees back home . . . ? And they asked again if this was really the General. . . . That man was all powerful . . . ! And why such refined hands . . . ? asked Chepe, in his childlike way.

Then the General departed, accompanied by his entourage. The reservists remained in silence, astonished by the strange scene. It had been like the appearance and disappearance of a god.

After a moment, the Sargent said: "You are blessed! Don't wash your hand touched by the General . . . ! You are blessed, and with pay . . . and before you go, leave something for your Sargent, who is sad, without a cent. . . ."

The men did as he asked. The Sargent collected what he needed for his celebration. A patriotic celebration, to celebrate the General's visit.

JUAN DE SENA DIDN'T know what to do. And now . . . ? He is free. Is it true what Corporal Bijo said, that the General was going to give each reservist a farm . . . ? He had thought about asking the General, but the guy had such a serious face. . . .

Behind them was the savannah, with its loneliness. That afternoon many men crossed it. Some were dressed in khaki, others in a coarse blue material, a soldier's plunder, miserable old rags they'd been given so they wouldn't arrive naked at their homes.

The wind fled. Faster than it does at twilight. Was it fleeing these men? Was it afraid of these men . . . ?

Stars go out above the savannah. You cannot see the walking men, whose bare feet split the clods of earth in every direction. They have money. Money given to them by the General who had ordered the Cutting. Their pay: ten pesos!

"The General was dressed like a god!"

"With a boss like that, I'm off to Haiti in two days!"

"The Major finished . . . we the bosses now . . . the General said. . . . We be the bosses now . . . the reservists. . . ."

"The Governor finish now. . . . They make me work without pay, like something borrowed . . . ! To build a road on his estate. . . . That's done with, my friend! . . . We the boss!"

"We the boss . . . ! No Major, no *Guaidia* tell us to do! The General say."

"Okay, we rich. The judge he finished. . . . I don't have to pay nothing for that little girl I stole days back . . . !"

"An me, running from Nebó the Spaniard . . . 'cause of two little cow I take. . . . He done finish threaten me with the public defender. . . . I a boss."

"Go on where the Spaniard and tell 'em. . . ."

"And me, yesterday I see Puzzo, the Italian, who have me down for two pigs I take. That Italian a thief, steal from everyone he sell to, and don't even pay those who work his land . . . and he say he gonna put me down with the defender, for two little pig. . . . I saw him and I tell him . . . he all fine, running to his house. . . . I a boss."

"An' me, needing two mountain sticks of Juanico Riva, that damn old man, harder than a *candelón* tree. . . . An' me without nothing. . . . If I enter the forest he send the defender after . . . and my house falling down without that wood. . . . You betta know it: I Anacleto Roldán, boss. . . . We done here now . . . !"

You couldn't see the faces of those who were speaking. Far away, you could hear strains of merengue in the night:

Heroine, tolalá . . .
Belongin' t' Sanche, tolalá . . .

26

Other men came to Dajabón now. They were the recruits from city lowlife. Also landless peasants without jobs, sentenced as "vagrants." These men would come to settle in Dajabón and its surroundings. They brought these "vagrants" in army trucks, like cattle. They arrived when all the cattle were gone and the mountain wind had turned the remains of the shacks and men to nitrate.

When the army trucks left, La China came to Dajabón. She bore that name so common in any dive, where there's always a China. This China asked everyone if they'd seen her man: Cholo El Colorao, whom they'd lured to these parts with the promise of a parcel replete with coffee plants. In the hills, the coffee plantations are abandoned. The berries are falling to the ground. There is no Haitian labor to gather that fruit and take it to Dajabón, to Don Lauterio's thieving hands. The vast fields are ripe with fruit. There are no laborers. The government is going to give all those riches to Dominicans. That's why they've rounded up lumpen. And prisoners.

How did La China get here? We don't know. But nothing gets in the way of the whore who emigrates with the swallows. She walks, comes in a truck, in a cart, or even in a car, although she doesn't pay her way. It's the same with my country's soldiers. They hitch a ride through charity or fear. Like La China, they change carriages, and finally arrive at their far-off destination.

Her partner, Cholo El Colorao, delinquent emissary from La Vega, remembers he's been in jail five times. Later he has been to the capital, and couldn't enroll in the army. He longed to be a lieutenant.

"Compay . . . I like the *Guaidia*! They get where to stay and a car . . . ! I gonna join up! Don' be a fool!"

"My friend . . . what *Guaidia*, what game. . . . I who play with Mililo, the one playing the three-string, and with blind Guazuma in the Bermúdez Orchestra. . . . General Piro Estrella he love our music . . . and General Trujillo himself, and we play at Cuesta Colorá. . . . What I like is the music . . . working with pick and shovel: well, that's for jail-birds. You ever seen a nightingale with machete, Compay Bolo? We had us our *orquestra*, the Benefactor Orchestra. . . . I ain't gonna work in them mountains . . . ! Mountain, they for the bird . . . ! What I like is strum my guitar, like when old Nico Lora break out that merengue and get the dead to dancing. . . ."

And he breathed deep, thinking of that merengue, hot as the earth at Villa Lobos. Sweet as its women.

"But . . . what to do . . . ?"

Perucho, from Guayubín, wasn't a musician. He sold lottery tickets

"Who say I wanna work in a field . . . ? I sell lottery ticket. I'm good with selling in the week, on Ei Soi Street. . . ." And he reminisces: "Adds up to twenty-one . . . twenty-one. . . . The Virgin . . . ! Adds up to twenty-one. . . ."

LIKE LA CHINA, other prostitutes arrived at Dajabón and went on to Loma de Cabrera. They and their menfolk saved their money there.

Every day, new mobs of dirty men descended from the official trucks. They were covered in mud. Some bore signs of mange from the humid dungeons where they'd been sent by judges who'd never spent two hours in a creole prison. The judges only jailed the poor.

Tenant farmers and prisoners arrived in the last trucks. The tenant farmers were sad, disgusted, and stared back at the road along which they'd been brought like cattle.

The government dispenses the cultivated land. Prisoners and tenant farmers. Vagrants from all the cities are suddenly landowners now, tenant farmers on our border.

"I . . . I WAS RUNNING a gambling house for Major Caraballo and he give me good tip every day. . . . And now he sends me here . . . ! 'Cause I don't got no idea. . . . Damn . . . ! What have black ever done to me . . . ? This ain't my thing . . . !"

Then he looked around, and added: "And can't even speak . . . 'cause they pick me up right here . . . !"

This Medardo Patricio remembered the tough land of La Joya—land as dangerous as a dagger—and his neighborhood concubine. Manuela Hard-as-a-Piston. Under his breath, he cursed the government for giving him land he doesn't want, still being cultivated by Haiti.

"This for the birds . . . or for the blacks . . . ! But I no bird. . . . I want little enough . . . let 'em keep their fields. . . . I getting outa here . . . !"

THE GOVERNMENT HAD POPULATED the land with delinquents and the hungry. Contrasts. The latest arrivals wanted to return to city misery. In contrast, the riches are here: Grass. Mangoes. Avocado groves. Miles of them. Green and black banana fields. There are yuccas in the furrows, like women giving birth. The mob has devoured these riches. But they haven't planted. They've come with their city weariness. Lowlife, people of the night, but for whom night life is the great life: alcohol, vice. Idle prostitutes, ghostly, like skinny dogs.

These delinquent mobs describe another aspect of the drama. As there are no more cows or calves to steal, the men are fighting over the best parcels of land.

Every night the crime claims new victims. Each afternoon the new settlers, already living on fertile fields they themselves don't work, use their fists to argue about which are best. The military patrol shows up. And metes out "justice." The patrol shoots the guilty settler right then and there.

Summary justice is typical of this part of the country. This was what happened yesterday afternoon. Bartolín, the guy from Juan Gómez, defended the plot that had previously been planted by Sambá the Haitian. He wasn't satisfied with the one that had belonged to black Dadá, who had given it to Corporal Bijo. On Dadá's land there is nothing left but foxtail and scrub brush. Mangy land, Bartolín said. He wanted Sambá's piece. In the ensuing struggle, he killed the other musician, who happened to be the owner of the better land, the one with green banana fields that hadn't been planted by any of them.

Later, they executed Bartolín. Both parcels remained empty. Cholo El Colorao looked at them and said: "Damn! Yucca sure expensive here . . . !" Later La China showed up with a plate with two pieces of yucca boiled in salt water. She was seminude. On the border, there are no *pargos*—clients. Loneliness forces her to go hungry and stay loyal to Cholo El Colorao.

"Yeah . . . not much yucca. . . . Cholo . . . ! You gotta plant some!"

But Cholo isn't thinking about working the land, and remains silent. He thinks like the rest of them: Flee! Go back to the city, to the bar, to alcohol and the night!

Poor whore, following her man. Like her, others. Are they sorry . . . ? Could hunger have changed them?

They followed their men, out of a combination of loyalty and a vagabond spirit that was eager to explore that land. Savage whore, dirty as the river bed, like her man a child of this river. With each whore came another mouth to feed. She too provided a dose of morphine to those men's apathetic spirits. La China and all the Chinas who are here now live hungry beneath the old awnings left by the Haitians.

All the while, the parcels got smaller. Each day there was less yucca. Haiti returned in the night. Those who passed through Cholo El Colorao's and La China's plot last night were like swine. Like any good matron, La China complained about the thieves: they finished off the yucca, the banana field, and made off with the little piglet!

HAITI CAME IN THE NIGHT. The thieves had silken feet. Sometimes a settler would wake. The next day, a head could be seen on the road. Whose was it . . . ? No one asked. It was the night. It was Haiti.

NOW THERE'S DETERMINATION IN the struggle: for a plot of land. Frontier land. The vagrant Medardo Patricio and Cholo El Colorao are in this fight. . . . Also, La China, Lola Güano, and Pancha Three in One. No one works. Everyone eats. La China sleeps all the time, because in the cities lowlife whores don't sleep and barely manage to eat. This China hardly knows how to cook, accustomed as she is to eating from nighttime street stalls. La China belongs to Medardo now. She left Colorao.

Medardo fell silent. That night he decided to watch over what was left of the yucca. In the middle of the night, behind the dry cornfield, he fought with black Natalí, who was shouting about this being his field and he was hungry. Midnight echoes with the words of men fighting with machetes. Medardo appeared lifeless the following morning. Natalí made off with all the yucca. La China doesn't know how to cry. On the border, they bury men where they fall. No need to bring Medardo to the farmhouse.

La China is like a wild bird now. She leaves the farm. She walks in the night, because she has almost no clothes, and the midday sun ravages her body. She got far, far away. Now she lives with a prisoner, Compay Santos. La China knows how to pick them: "I come over here 'cause the land good . . . ! And the men like to work . . . ! And my second husband, Medardo, left me naked as Christ."

IF CROSSES WERE TREES, this land would be a forest. A cross for Medardo? What for? No one would care. A cross would be like one more mango tree, in the midst of a vast grove. . . .

Despite all the wealth, the mobs that had come by truck to Dajabón were seminaked, hungry. Haiti had come in the night and harvested by the light of the moon.

The border: daggers, drought, cattle, hunger. . . . With all the wealth of forest and field. . . . And all the while, a constant flowering of crosses. There were no crosses, only red sticks in the night. The fires send ash—the ash of men—onto the clear breeze that blows across the fields of La Línea.

THAT AFTERNOON, UPON MY return from Loma de la Garrapata, I sat beneath the mango tree where they carved up Samuel, the black man who planted the estate that is now Cholo El Colorao's home. I thought about Haiti's destiny. I thought about the Dominican Republic's destiny. Meanwhile, Don David, the government's dispenser of land, kept telling me his nauseating stories of beheadings. Don David went on and on. His stories were long, like that immense extension of mango trees and avocado groves.

THE FOREST RETURNED to the land once worked by Haiti. Their crops depleted, those thugs on the border only made cassava bread from what remained of the yucca. These bakers were forgotten by the governments now. Chemo Natividad was one of the many bakers.

This is the dialogue between Chemo Natividad and a pure blood from Juan Nazario, who had returned to Haiti.

"This yucca ours . . . ! I planted it . . . ! When my country here . . . !"

"So . . . you one of them . . . ? I gonna bury you with your yucca!"

An aggressive voice, like that of a beast.

They clash. Again. Both machetes meet flesh.

"Shithead Haitian . . . ! Devilish Haitian . . . ! This land mine . . . !"

"I Dominican too . . . !"

After the fight, Chemo Natividad was the only one to be seen. He comes from the river. Chemo Natividad has cow pies plastered on the broad wounds that bleed and bleed without stopping.

That same night, those on the other side of the river found a sack they thought contained the yucca the pureblood had gone looking for in the field that used to be his. When they opened the sack, they found a head. Juan Nazario's other children look at the sack like squalid dogs. They don't speak. El Masacre runs alongside them. Is it horrified too?

THIS IS THE MARKET where yucca brings the highest prices in my country. Here is a tragic calendar. The rural teacher told me the story:

Monday: Samba Pié . . . Tuesday: Michel Jean . . . Wednesday: Fenelón Dois . . . Thursday: Samuel, the milkman . . . Friday: Perico, the carpenter . . . Saturday: Timué Dis . . . Sunday: Antuán Salé and Sampré, the shoemaker . . .

And so the weeks go by. And the months. A dagger harvest. As intense as the sugarcane harvests at the mills. The victims were carrying mangoes and yuccas when they fell. There, behind those hills, they were waiting for them. Hungry. Desperate. Misery of a single coin: the round moon that floats above the water of El Masacre, poor little river . . . flowing by. . . .

CORPORAL RIVAS ASKS THE small landowner: "What was that poor guy carrying?"

"Ah, my lord . . . poor black . . . ! He was taking his few mangoes over Haiti. . . ."

Corporal Rivas counted: he was carrying fifty mangoes.

Then he said: "Take those mangoes to Lieutenant Bolo's pigs, back of them barracks there. . . ."

The afternoons are a leaden gray that make me think of those "rains" by our illustrious painter Suro. It seems to me that those great big stars are crying these dramas. Lieutenant Bolo's pigs are devouring the mangoes. They are content. On the other hand, no one notices that these mangoes, these riches, this fruit of La Línea, cost Haiti its heart. I said it before: Haiti is trading hearts for mangoes. And it's summer now.

I HEARD VOICES IN the night. After a few months, trucks arrived once more in Dajabón. The government ordered the return to the cities of those mobs of smelly thugs and whores who had spent a year on the border. They returned in tatters, almost naked. But they were happy: they would return to their alcohol, their night! There was a terrible solitude on the land then. Two sure things would return to this latitude: the forest. And Haiti.

27

I'm still here in these parts. I am a mute witness. A complicit witness. My conscience is hounding me. What is my duty? . . . To accuse? I should leave! And why remain here in this village, having taken refuge in this house, isolated, immersed in the solitude of its nights, on the immense savannah? Sometimes I try to read the Judicial Bulletin, beneath the weak light of the kerosene lamp. It is the official magazine of my country's Supreme Court, and I don't want to remain ignorant of our jurisprudence. I have no one to talk to. The village houses shut down at an early hour, and I've gone to Mistress Francina's shabby inn. I detest her inquisitive and duplicitous nature. They say she is a government spy, ever ready to betray the functionaries who criticize these events.

My companion, the judge, is a good man who has taken to daily poisoning himself with drink. As soon as the trials of those occasional crimes that take place here end—a few robberies, stabbings, kidnappings of young girls—the judge goes to visit an army officer who belongs to an aristocratic family from Puerto Plata, an elegant man who repudiates all this, and who also bears it by remaining permanently drunk. I am alone.

My only comfort are the letters I receive from Angela, the schoolteacher who is my lady friend. Those letters also shock me. In my country's capital, she has gone everywhere in search of work. Despite her excellence as a secretary, all doors have been closed to her. Many pretty girls tell the same story.

Clever suitors had sought her out. The principal among these had been a Minister of State. He had found the neighborhood where Angela lived, and the powerful man's luxury automobile had parked several times in front of her house. The first time, he'd sent his chauffeur with an enticing message: he wanted to see her about a job. Angela had gone to see him. The Minister, elegant and reeking of cologne, looked as if he had been dressed by a London tailor. On both hands, he wore bright rings set with precious stones. He feigned interest in her need to work. He asked her to return in two days. Angela went to the Ministry again. When she got there, the doorman had a message: the Minister was waiting for her at his country home and an automobile was waiting to take her there.

Angela was taken aback, but quickly decided to decline. She made an excuse. She told the doorman she preferred to see him the following day. She didn't return. But it seemed the Minister was "committed" to getting together with this interesting prey. He managed to see Angela again.

Cunningly he tried to give her money, but she refused. From that moment on, the girl was stalked: at home and in the street. The Minister even got female agents to invite her to parties; he tried every ruse. When he failed, he handed down something like a dictum: she would not find work in any office. This order is carried out implacably, and even involves the private sector. She is unable to find work anywhere.

I have had to help her out, at the cost of insulting her dignity. I have sent her money with my friend Doctor Vélez, who only recently got out of prison, where he had been confined because of his dissent standing up to the regime.

There is more anguish in each letter. I must escape! Escape this nightmare. Valiantly, Angela tells me: "We must escape at all costs, even if you must board a ship and go away, even if I lose you."

Rereading these lines, I feel accused. I can see that Angela Vargas, the little ex-teacher from El Almácigo, has a strength of character I lack. These thoughts will not leave me in peace, and I spend long nights unable to sleep. Then I remember that judge who fled. He could no longer resist his degrading role of the judge in a tragic operetta. He fled. And they went after him. Major Ozuna came to my house to question me. A black man who smokes a long pipe and drives a luxurious automobile, and whom I knew as a gardener at the home of a Minister who was a friend of my father's.

With proconsular airs, the Major questioned me. I was supposed to know about the judge's ideas, where he lived, what he talked about, what his plans were. He told me he'd already been denounced by everyone in the secret police and some said he was a communist. He was an ungrateful wretch. The generous General had honored him with a high-level secret mission, and he'd repaid him with treason. The Major warned me of treason's price in this regime. The General's hand, aristocratic and elegant as the reservist Loreto de la Cruz experienced it, was an iron fist when it came to those who showed the slightest disloyalty.

Major Ozuna cursed me loudly, and I could hear how he hated me: I had never attended his parties. Nor the Captain's. I always declined invitations to Mistress Sebastiana's house, where she gave her grand events and dinners, and where the General frequently stayed. I was the renegade, the only one who didn't go. Everyone accused me. "We must keep an eye on that public prosecutor . . . he seems hostile. . . ." Mistress Sebastiana seemed to be passing judgment, just as she had previously passed judgment on my lady friend, the little schoolteacher. One day I received a piece of advice from the Major. He came to my house under the guise of friendship. He brought a bottle of whiskey. The gesture disgusted me, but I accepted out of courtesy. I was wary, and pretended to drink. What is the man doing . . . ? I wondered.

When he was almost drunk, he embraced me.

"Attorney . . . I want you to do me a favor. . . . Go to Mistress Se-
bastiana's house . . . and bring the teacher from El Almácigo. . . .
It's in both your interests. The General will be at the feast of San
Fernando. . . ."

I understood the trap he was laying for me. Quickly I responded:
"Of course, we'd be delighted, Major Ozuna. . . . We'll be there. . . ."

This man, to whom everyone in the village except me paid tribute,
had figured out a way to destroy us. In his reports—every military
official had to report on everything going on in his jurisdiction—he
used the most damaging formula: he had let it be known that the
little teacher, a woman of utmost integrity, was the attorney's concubine. . . . This accusation had appeared in her file again and again,
until it was enough for her frustrated stalker to have her fired from
her job.

He also earned merits with Mistress Sebastiana, who wanted to get
back at the teacher for having spurned her invitations.

I knew all this, and knew I was being watched and accused. The
Major's crude words left me indifferent. I didn't know anything about
the judge who had escaped.

I ponder all this through my nights of insomnia. I also remember
when Angela Vargas came to see me in Dajabón, on her way back to
the capital after she had lost her job. She went to see me at my office.
We spoke only briefly. But the visit ended with a kiss of profound love,
made more dramatic in the light of such tragedy. She said she would
send me her address. I advised prudence, and that she shouldn't trust
anyone. Then we sealed our love by my giving her all the notes I
had taken regarding the massacre. I asked her to keep them safe, no
matter what. If anything happened to her, she should give them to
my mother in sealed envelopes. Carrying those notes was like carrying a time bomb that could explode at any moment. If they fell into
the hands of the secret police, those notes could bring death upon us
both. I would be vilified for being disloyal to the regime. She would
disappear, never to be seen again.

Since then, I've received numerous letters from Angela. She is a
fighter. She cannot imagine not fighting, even if she perishes in the

struggle. More than love letters, hers are programs of resistance. And she fills me with hope. Above all else, she urges me to leave this place. I imagine her there, in constant danger in the capital. She lives by selling pieces of embroidery she and her mother make. At night, after she finishes her needlework, she reads. In her most recent letters she has been asking about my health. I've been suffering from high fevers. Fevers are common here in the village, because of the mosquitos that breed in El Masacre, in the shallows where there is no current. The village is drenched with sun and mosquitoes; and in the springtime with gnats—tiny winged insects that swarm about, getting in your mouth, nose, eyes.

ONE OF MY ILLNESS'S side effects is insomnia. I begin to feel feverish and delirious here in my shack, aided only by Bitín, the aging servant at the Court. I feel like I am sinking to the bottom of a deep sea. Where am I going . . . ? Death must feel like this.

A journey to the bottom, until I lose consciousness, until I am no more than a thing, an anchor detached from its boat, in the middle of the ocean.

I keep descending to the depths. Where am I . . . ?

And then I awaken, semiconscious. I place my hand on the cot upon which I have been sleeping. I see the mosquito net. I see the good-natured face of the village woman who has brought me an infusion of tea.

"Judge: You talk a lot . . . ! About a war with Haitians . . . !"

Then I realize I've had a delirious dream in which I've seen the past like a moving picture.

28

I should take notes on my feverish visions while abandoned here in the village. Angela should add them to the notes of mine she already has.

The old black priest came around. He sat down beside me. He began to speak to me. Then other figures approached my bed, sinister figures enveloped in shadow.

"I am Saint Louverture . . . Toussaint! I was a slave and a coachman. Look at my hands; they drip blood. . . . I exacted payment from the whites for their injustice, in the profits of the oppressor: injustice. The French bosses slit the throats of my brothers, the blacks. For the least complaint, they cut them up. Their dogs, the mastiffs brought by Rochambeau, Napoleon's general, ate black men's flesh. . . . Commander de la Tortuga warned Rochambeau that he wouldn't sell rations for cash. He had to feed his mastiffs black meat. . . . They forced the black man to suffer the wheel. They cut him up without tears, with an ax as if they were chopping down a tree.

"Sugar, coffee, cocoa, indigo. The black men produced them for the whites of France, who paid them with lashings. . . . But look at their ashes. Look at the corpses of the whites. They have gone up in flame along with their cane fields. . . . I have put one over on them all, English, French, Spaniards, and they were all the same: men who only wanted more and more riches. . . . I conquered them all. . . . This land is mine. . . . I have vanquished the French whites. . . . And now I will vanquish the Spanish whites of Santo Domingo. Although I am a Christian, I will slit their throats. I will kill their women, their pretty children, and demolish their altars. All those who live in the part of Santo Domingo still governed by the Spanish will die. . . . The Island is one and indivisible. . . . Haiti is bordered only by the sea. . . ."

"I am Dominga Núñez, a Spanish woman from Santo Domingo. Insolent black! Beware if you touch me with your cane, in this plaza where you have gathered everyone so you can behead us! Learn some manners to deal with Spaniards! Kill, behead right now if you wish. . . . But we pay you no heed!!"

"I am Jean Philippe Dau . . . ! I want to drink blood! Blood! More blood! I want to drink it mixed with rum. The blood of white Spaniards! Kill, my soldiers! Kill all these Spaniards who hate us because we are black and they are slaveholders. . . . Give me blood, I want to wash my face with blood, in honor of Haiti's black gods. . . . Here, in San Carlos, not even ashes will remain. . . . Shoot, Haitian soldiers . . . kill even the last of the children. . . ."

"Don, I am innocent. I am Don Antonio España. I work my land, I look after my slaves who are like children to me. You will see that my slaves have no interest in your freedom, in your liberation. . . . Why do you murder me, here on my estate, where cane and tobacco grow and where I elevate my heart to God? What did you come here for, preying on everything, killing us all, burning our homes and stealing our cattle . . . ? And now your troop of Dahomeyans pierce my chest with your spears, rip out my still living heart and devour it . . . !"

"I too am black, like you . . . but I am Spanish. . . . Is that why your saber has slashed my heart in two . . . ?"

"Beg pardon, ferocious Haitians. . . . What crime have I committed . . . ? Do you kill me only because I am white?"

"Ferocious Haitian cannibals . . . ! Respect the old ones, although you kill all those who are young. . . . You didn't even spare the churches . . . ! Look at the altars and the bishops' staffs, stained with innocent blood. Kill me . . . ! I am Father Juan Vásquez, the one who hates you, drinkers of blood. . . . Pile more wood here, upon the altar. Bring more wooden pews, more saints carved of wood. Bring more wood. Bring more fuel to burn me alive, inside this House of God. . . . He will make you pay. You will burn my body like a wick. I must accompany my faithful, those you have already assassinated, without respect for women, old people and children, here in this church, on this day which is the feast of Pentecost. . . . Burn! Free my miserable body. . . . Damned blacks, drinkers of blood!"

"Savages . . . ! Why do you throw the children into the air to skewer them on your sharpened bayonets . . . ?"

"Oh, brothers . . . ! Behold the ruins of Santiago . . . ! All is ash. . . . We flee in the night to the rugged mountains. . . . Only we four men are still alive, after today's massacre. The black hordes have destroyed the churches, the houses, the shrines. They have beheaded our parents and friends. Only we four remain. We flee in the night."

"Where do you come from? I flee Moca. The people have been burned alive. The men from La Vega come on foot, among animals and cattle droppings, tied together like cows. They will strangle them or take them to Haiti as slaves. . . . Dessalines only wanted more and more blood. We are fleeing. But where . . . ?"

"I am the mulatto Serapio Reynoso. I died at the Ambush, holding off nine thousand cannibals. . . . Santiago has disappeared beneath the knife!"

"Dominicans . . . I am Dessalines, owner of Haiti . . . ! Only one way remains to you: death by steel and the burning of your haciendas. . . . I will drive all your cattle and other animals to Haiti. Fire will mark my path. Where no fields, no cities remain. Your fate is to die beneath the boots of Haitian soldiers. . . . No old people, children, or women will escape . . . ! Not a single white will set foot on this land. Haiti . . . a land for blacks alone . . . !"

"And I . . . am Faustin, the emperor Soulouque. . . . You will die, Dominicans . . . ! My sword blade will find you, no matter where you hide. I will hunt you down in the mountains, like wild animals. . . . Haitian steel will kill you all. . . ."

THIS IS WHERE MY delirious fever ends. I woke in the middle of the night. A profound night. It always seemed to me to be the bottom of a tragic ocean in which the water isn't green but red: blood. I opened the window of my shack where I was alone, in the dark of a frontier night. Impenetrable darkness and profound desolation. I could hear only the screams of Don Panchito, the crazy one, my neighbor, who agonized for fourteen nights, screaming like a dog and occasionally squealing like a pig, crowing like a rooster in the middle of the night. Don Panchito, the killer! (They say that when he died four green snakes slithered from his mouth. And when they tried to grab and kill them, they spoke like humans. In Patois!) I looked up at the sky and saw the pure light of the stars. Those brilliant stars gave me a sense of relief. The morning cleared little by little over the brown meadow on the outskirts of the village. It surprised me, meditating upon the history I was witnessing with my own eyes, written in letters of blood, and that other pitiless history of tyranny and crimes committed by the Haitians that I had learned at school in my childhood.

29

After my escape, I have looked for her unsuccessfully. One night I abandoned the village of Dajabón, pretending to be a servant of Justice. A friend's car was waiting for me outside town. He was a traveling salesman and unafraid to help me flee, a young man whose father had been assassinated by the dictatorship. He didn't fear associating himself with my crime, that of skipping out on my position at the border.

And here in the city, with the secret police constantly in my pursuit, I have looked day and night but haven't found her. Where is my lady friend, Angela Vargas? She had left my notes on the border with my mother.

Her letters arrived like clockwork, every week. First, they were written on romantic paper, faintly perfumed. Letters penned on rose-colored sheets upon which there might be a drawing of hearts pierced by Cupid's arrow. Later the letters arrived on ordinary paper. Finally, I received a couple on cheap, brown construction stock. Her letters recorded the tide of her misery. And each one was filled with love and tragedy.

Now she worked as a slave in a sweatshop where she made crude work clothes beside other operators, some of them skinny and sick. Most of them were young mothers, forced to stop nursing their young. Others left small children at home in red-light districts, at the mercy of drunken delinquents. The sweatshop work was monotonous. It was hard to breathe. The only word spoken was "misery."

It was in that world that Angela Vargas labored, pursued by a pack of powerful men who wanted to prostitute her. They had purposefully closed all doors in education, her chosen profession. Even in that situation, Angela wrote me sweet love letters, filled with a dignity rare among women of her age. I came to feel ashamed. There was such a contrast between my cowardliness, yoked to the tyranny, and the heroic life of that delicate, beautiful young woman, sharing the disgrace of those sweatshop workers.

In one of her letters she told me of her mother's death. She died of consumption and moral martyrdom. A clandestine women workers' union paid for the humble funeral. The letter brought tears but also fortitude. As always, it was full of advice, urging me to "be a man" and turn my back on the dictatorship. She showed me a way out: the sea, a foreign land, "so you may retrieve your manly identity."

I could no longer stand the confrontation: my fear for her safety and the challenge of breaking my chains that was evident in each of her letters. I made my decision.

I WENT TO HER NEIGHBORHOOD, but no one knew where she had gone. One day she'd escaped, just as I had from that distant border province. Where...? No neighbor had any idea. She had left everything—her few possessions: a small bed, some crude wooden furniture. She took a picture of her mother and her Virgen of Altagracia. She had left at night. They had seen her around the port area. She was walking arm in arm with a Danish captain who spoke Spanish.

I suffered from an absurd jealousy then. Had she abandoned me? Faced with my inability to liberate myself, could she have indulged in a final infidelity?

From that moment, I began frequenting the port. I went there constantly. I wanted to find out something, some information. Useless. Then I decided to pay a visit to Doctor Vélez, our friend who lived on the outskirts of the city, surrounded by books and trees. Vélez had been a spiritual refuge for Angela. Like her, he was talented and full of dignity. Persecuted by the regime, he had been in prison numerous times. Angela's rebellious spirit found solace in him.

When I arrived, he received me nervously and with these words: "She left . . . forever! She was tired of waiting . . . ! She escaped on a Danish cargo ship that was supposed to take her to Venezuela. Before going to the port, pretending to be a prostitute so as to confound those who were following her, she came to see me and told me to tell you to go to see Doctor Fradíquez."

The news hit me like a bolt of lightning. I felt cowardly, frustrated. And I had gotten to the point of feeling jealous of Angela, who was a model of virtue. I fell silent before the doctor, who looked at me with his genial cross-eyed expression from behind dark glasses. I hardly heard his pressing words, urging me as Angela had: "Take freedom's road! Be brave like Angela! You are young. If I were your age, I wouldn't be here!"

Then he added: "And now you must be careful, because the hounds are looking for you, day and night . . . I know that Major Ozuna sent a file to the government, accusing you of being a communist and an enemy of the regime . . . for having left your job in Dajabón. . . . The secret police have been to your mother's house on several occasions . . . They're after you. You should only go out after dark. . . ."

Doctor Vélez hid me at his country home. I only went out at night to see my mother and younger brothers, all of whom depended on the bread I was able to provide them.

LIKE A TRUE WISE MAN, Doctor Fradíquez lived in a simple house. He had a Mexican wife and two precious daughters. The house was filled with books and more books. They were on shelves, on the tables, on desks. Books marked with thin strips of paper, because the doctor read several books at a time and took lots of notes. His was an organized mind, a vibrant intelligence, a permanent scholar, but above all a good man.

A native who nonetheless had lived many years outside the country, he was a humanist who figured among the most outstanding professors in North America, Chile, and Argentina. After achieving significant fame as a professor, critic, linguist, and literary and philosophical scholar, he had returned to the country he had never forgotten, haunted by a melancholy for those now departed. He had accepted a position at the Ministry of Education, offered to him by the government. But very soon he realized how vitiated the atmosphere was, an atmosphere unacceptable to a man whose whole life had unfolded in places of freedom and dignity. He saw the dictatorship's claws coming ever closer, even to the threshold of his own home. He was aware of the chorus of opportunists who claimed he was cool toward the regime. They ridiculed him publicly, accusing him of disaffection, and said his teaching methods were inept.

Undeterred, Doctor Fradíquez put up with that disloyal attack. Meanwhile, he prepared his definitive departure from his beloved homeland, to which he had returned crowned with laurels and scorning offers from the best universities because he wanted to help rebuild his country.

WHEN I ARRIVED, he received me with the serene smile of a good and simple man. He knew his house was being watched, so he wanted to speak to me quickly.

"Everything is arranged. The young lady should be in Venezuela. The master of the Colombian school ship, a great seaman who was a student of mine at Harvard, is waiting for you. You must go at midnight on Wednesday, to San Diego port. Wear a white shirt, without a jacket, and a red tie, which will be the signal. But first, in the afternoon, send me your clothing with a sailor who will come for it here. The ship is headed for Buenos Aires. You will disembark there. The commodore already has instructions on how to get in touch with my friends in that city who will provide you with false documents until I can join you.... You must leave everything behind...! Be strong...! Strong...!" He uttered these last words with great force, in an exalted voice I had never heard him use before. His usually serene face was contorted. He fell silent, and then continued: "Forget everything...! Even your mother...! And your orphan siblings...! Everyone...! To Buenos Aires! And wait for me there. I will connect you with a publishing house. You will live with dignity...!"

And he added, in his usual calm teaching voice: "I have faith in you. Why shouldn't you be one of America's great free pens...?"

Then he abruptly cut the conversation short. He looked outside and said: "Midnight Wednesday...! Go on, leave...! I see a man coming who spies on this house every night...! Out!"

30

Time passed rapidly. I was filled with confusion. One thought obsessed me: "Wednesday at midnight!" That's when my liberation would begin. I remembered the fraternal but imperious words of Doctor Fradíquez: I must forget everyone. Even my elderly mother and young siblings, for whom I was the only support!

But finally, I accepted the sacrifice. I decided to hide my intentions. I pretended to send my clothes to the laundry. The Colombian sailor had carried out our plans with great precision. He had retrieved my suitcase from Doctor Fradíquez's house and taken it to the ship.

That night my mother had an attack of nerves. It had begun in the afternoon, when a bailiff arrived at the house with a sheaf of legal papers. They ordered our eviction, because we were behind with the rent. I stayed with my mother all that night. I finally convinced her to take a sleeping pill, and she fell into a deep sleep. I went to bed but couldn't sleep. My heart was beating in unison with my cheap watch. As if it too was counting the hours.

Around eleven, as everyone in the house slept, I quietly got up. I looked upon the faces of each of my siblings. I spent a long time gazing at my mother's angelic countenance.

I thought: "Abandoned ones!!"

"Abandoned, miserable, with nothing to eat!

"Tomorrow they will come to insult your mother! Then the bailiff will return and throw her few possessions into the street. With everyone looking on. And they will say: Her oldest son abandoned her!"

Mentally, I reread the sentence brought that afternoon by the bailiff.

"Eviction! But where to go . . . ?

"Abandonment!

"You love yourself more than you love your mother . . . !

"You love yourself more than you love your helpless brothers!!!"

These thoughts went through my mind in rapid succession, in a matter of seconds. But I gathered my strength and continued dressing. I remembered the hour: twelve midnight! At San Pedro port!

I was about to leave. But just before that, as I moved toward the door, my mother seemed to awaken. I almost changed my mind. Fortunately, she hadn't completely awakened. I got as far as the living room. From there I could see them all again, all the abandoned ones. I cried. I left.

I made my way through the streets, avoiding the nightly police patrol. As I reached Colón Plaza, I heard the old bells on the Municipal Palace's clock. It was eleven thirty. The sound of those bells produced fear in me, almost panic. Why? At that moment, I felt like a delinquent. I had wanted to flee. But where . . . ? I wanted to retrace my steps and go back. But at the same time, I knew I had to get to the nearby port. I walked unsteadily, like a drunk.

Just as I reached Isabel la Católica street, close to the port, a military patrol stopped me. They were looking for a communist lawyer. According to Major Ozuna, it might be me. They asked for my identification papers. I had my false ID to avoid being caught. I explained. They hesitated. They asked my name again, although they had read it on my documents:

"*I am Fredio Gimbernat!* You are looking for someone else!" (I tried to avoid the yellow gaze of the chief of patrol, a dirty gaze like that of the soldiers who kill people on the border. Perhaps he had served there. Or in one of the tyranny's prisons. It's all the same.) The patrol chief looked at me again: "The guy we're looking for looks a lot like you. . . . Let's go down to the station . . . !"

I begged. I explained. I was out, I said, looking for medicine for my mother, who was gravely ill. Finally, inexplicably, they let me go. Almost a quarter of an hour had passed, precisely the time I needed to get to San Pedro port. I waited, discreetly, until the patrol was out of sight. When I began to walk again, the old clock struck once more. I don't know why those bells, which I'd heard in my childhood and throughout my life, filled me with such terror now. Quarter to twelve . . . ! But I was paralyzed! I must have acted like an idiot at that moment. I couldn't move. Now, feverishly, I remembered my mother. By now she would have gotten up, as she always did, to look through the house and at each of her children in their beds. She would have noticed my absence! What would she think . . . ?

I had abandoned her without resources, under threat of eviction, consigned in a sentence I had hidden by keeping the bailiff's papers from her.

And once again, I heard that voice in the night: "You are abandoning them!"

"You only think of yourself!

"They will put her out in the street!"

Then the last bell sounded. Midnight! And there I remained, paralyzed, confounded by what was happening. I couldn't move. I found myself rigid, in the dark, at the open gate to a colonial house. It began to rain hard. It was May. In that rain, in the middle of the night, I felt like the loneliest and vilest of men. Then I thought of Angela—the brave one—who had escaped on her own. And I felt like the most cowardly of men!

The rain continued. In the end, to justify my indecision I hoped it wouldn't stop. I felt bewildered, feverish. I spoke to myself. Then a drunk woman came to the gate, a streetwalker, one of those who wander the city all night long looking for customers. The place stank of the nauseous smell of rum. I could barely see her in the shadows. She thought she was alone. When she noticed me, the low-life woman approached and almost without a word offered to share her bottle. I pretended to drink. When she drew near, I saw her face in the dim light. It looked like a carnival mask, furrowed with premature wrinkles and knife scars. It was La China... she who had frequented the border farms, the musician Cholo El Colorao's concubine.

"What's your name...?" I asked her.

"They call me La China.... I'm running from the cops...! For that bottle, I cut a woman good... and they looking for me... they gonna look in the neighborhood... where the poor is, them dogs...."

When the rain stopped, the woman disappeared in the night. Poor China, I thought, less sad than me.

I continued to stand in the entranceway. Then another voice came to me, one I knew all too well from my nights of insomnia in the village of Dajabón. It goaded me persistently:

"Coward!

"Coward!

"Get out! Get out!"

Those two words finally sent me on my way. When I looked at the clock, it was one in the morning. I made a supreme effort and started to run. Quickly, I made it down the hill along Las Damas street. I got to San Pedro port. I stopped there. I waited. No one came to identify me by my red tie. I felt impotent, empty, light as a bird's feather. Then I walked to the dock. At that moment, from where I stood on the pier, I could see the ship that had just departed. It was making its way through the river channel. It passed the fort and began to raise the Dominican flag alongside the flag of Colombia. I had arrived too late!

I ran, then, to the esplanade that looks out upon the Caribbean. I could see the beautiful frigate, sailing, white, like a great gull, as she parted the waves of the Antilles. Desperate, like a departing lover, she saw my impotence. Mid-river, she had stopped for the usual ceremonial salute. At that moment, I wanted to jump in and swim out to her!

I stood there, enveloped in fog. I watched her go until I lost her along the line of the horizon!

Then I returned home, in the morning, accompanied by an intimate sense of shame and betrayal. My mother was waiting for me. I lied. To keep from having to make conversation and try to make my mother feel better, I fell into bed. An awkward lethargy descended upon me, something between sleep and wakefulness.

That dawn voice I heard in the village returned. It wouldn't stop its accusatory hammering: *"Coward! Coward!"*

31

Surrounded by filth and solitude, not knowing when my jailor will come and open the door. And so, I must write.

"I remember you, Pablo. When you appeared at my house—you were black, ugly, poor—Aunt Eloisa swatted you away like a fly. We snuck off to play in the courtyard, green with fruit trees, iridescent with exotic and native birds brought there by my father. Calm green shade, beautiful strings of carnations, water in the canals, a few statues. Mature cherry and cedar trees. You penetrated that stately courtyard like thieves enter the homes of the rich: with fear and hatred. You were afraid of Aunt Eloisa. One day you surprised me by saying: "You are rich!"

And you remained there, thinking. I couldn't know what you knew.

I asked: Who are the rich? I thought all men were equal. You knew they aren't. For me, the big house and its garden were also your home. That was when you told me you lived near the port, in a miserable shack you had to abandon when it rained because the river flooded everything. I remember you told me, when you heard Aunt Eloisa's piano: "How pretty the piano is. . . . At my house, we don't have a piano. . . ." You also told me: "I don't have a mother like you do. . . ." And you cried. "She lives with a new man now, at the refinery. He hits her every day. . . . The man works with the oxen and is always drunk. The man is strong, he hits my mother and sings to his oxen. . . . When I am older, I will kill that man. . . ." And you cried again.

I calmed you. I asked you to tell me what the refinery was like. Mornings are cold at the refinery. The cart driver gets up early. The oxen smell of fodder and molasses. The oxen are the only ones who eat. Neither the cart driver nor the field hand have anything to put in their mouths. A strong, cold wind blows in from the cane fields. The ox drivers drink rum. Then they forget and sing. Before he goes off with his cart, the strong man hits your mother, because she didn't sew his torn shirt, almost impossible to mend. I knew nothing of that world. You knew everything about it, and began to cry, again, in rage. I thought you even hated me. . . . Then Aunt Eloisa came and threw you out of the house: you were "a fly . . ." And I was left alone, without you. Pablo, without your stories of the refinery. . . . What did you do wrong, Pablo?

But now you are the minister, and you haven't come to the prison to see me. I remember your postcards from Paris and Geneva. You lusted after white women. In the last photo, you appeared to be sleeping in the arms of a voluptuous Dutch woman. In Geneva, you got revenge on Aunt Eloisa! I don't know if you've forgotten the ox driver's roundups, the ones you told me about; the mill in the morning cold and the cart driver's desolate dawns. You told me all that with an old man's composure. And your mother . . . ? Ah, yes . . . ! She died of consumption. Where is she . . . ? There is no cemetery at the refinery. Yes, Pablo, your happiness consists of forgetting. . . .

This is the port. The *Yumero* was a flying fish. There was a strong wind that night at Ozama, the river port. You must know, Aunt Eloisa, that I lived at the port ever since I missed the Colombian frigate that should have taken me to freedom. I had a single obsession: Angela! Angela free, and me a slave! In my dreams, in that dungeon at the port, I sensed Major Ozuna nearby, as if he was looking for me. I thought I could smell his mastiff breath, his beast's fangs, set to devour his prey. For Major Ozuna and those who believed as he did, I was "the communist," "the dangerous one." A serious crime, that of abandoning a job at the border!

And the port is a different country. Among its filth, among its delinquents, I detected a faint air of freedom, of self-defense. In that brownish conglomeration, at the waterfront, one can better hear the night's voice. Forgotten by everyone, even my mother! Free in that filth. Filth of animal shit, of the garbage from the port, asphalt, smoke, herring burning on the open grill, other fish. Filth in the torn cloth of old sails and rope worn down like the teeth of the fishing bosses—hairy, ferocious animals, drinkers, smokers.

And so eternally: gazing at the wind, at the night, at the tide. Eyes of a mountain cat with which to spy. Hands as hard as the nails in a ship, that take out their misery on the youngest, the apprentices. These don't have parents, or don't know them. Their new father, the boss, is always in a bad mood. Later they too will become bosses. And there will be a new group of beaten-down apprentices, who appear like green slime coating the sides of the barges.

Did he eat? Didn't he eat . . . ? It's all the same. Bad weather. Good wind. Unfurl the sail. Raise the boom. Tie the jib. The sea. That's freedom. And always misery. But I was better off there. Major Ozuna wouldn't come to the *Yumero*'s hold, my hiding place. The unasked question: "Which night . . . ? When will we flee . . . ?" I must not speak. Major Ozuna will not find me there, in that cargo hold, surrounded by rats and filth.

I looked through a hole. I saw the Captain, Alejandro Yanga's copper face. He did not speak. A sad thought might have hovered across his forehead, like a persistent fly. TISICA. Consumption! Meaning the same. And that was it, consumption. She was, they said, pretty, with olive skin and two long black braids. Higuemota, the Captain's daughter. Pretty in the hold, where only drunks come around. Consumption.

The Captain has no freight. He has no money. Consumption, without a doctor, humidity in the hold, until the river rises and we must abandon ship. The flies of thought hover: Consumption. If I had money, I wouldn't have to go as a hideaway to Venezuela with the

Chinese. They would pay for the cargo on the other end. Mamblé had made the arrangement and gone to see the fixer. Major Ozuna will run into me soon enough. "Wait." I am still in the *Yumero*'s hold, accompanied by rats. Wait! Bad weather. The river brought lots of garbage. Bad weather. Wait. Damned Chinese, poor guys. They will pay for them in Venezuela . . . consumption.

It was the man himself. Major Ozuna. He was down at the port, drunk, with a blonde woman. Was he looking for me . . . ? If Aunt Eloisa could see that blonde with black Major Ozuna's arm around her, she would die of repulsion.

It was the fault of Mamblé, the Captain's helper. On the high sea, across from Catalina Island, he killed the Chinese and threw them overboard to the sharks. First, when they were already dead he searched their bodies. They had no money! I looked at the Captain and at Mamblé. They were speechless. There wasn't any money. "Tísica." The deck was covered with yellow blood.

The guard—coastguard, military men—were nearby and called out: "Come on out. You are under arrest!"

What will become of Oguistén, the old Haitian who was at the port? They brought him in a truck and tossed him in a dumpster. Like some useless thing. Half-paralyzed, blind. He had lost his strength and sight in the cane fields. At the refinery, he'd probably become a nuisance. They got rid of him like they do with old oxen. He was half-crazy. At times, he muttered: *"A cuté le can . . . ! A cuté le can . . . !"* Maybe he was seeing oxen, cane carts, muddy fields, stalks of cane. Beneath the bridge, almost in the water. Oguistén has neither land nor homeland. Maybe he remembered. He crossed El Masacre many years ago. It wasn't hard. You can cross El Masacre on foot.

Yes, they were the same ones. Oguistén's brothers. From the port, I could see them going by in trucks, the kind they haul cattle in, to the eastern plantations. Shrieking and dirty. They carry roosters and parrots. They are parrots. They will cut cane like Oguistén, the Haitian who is now in the dumpster. Like Oguistén, they will escape the immigration police. Perhaps, in years to come, they will have their own dumpsters. Haitians go for fifteen pesos a head. A good deal.

Why do I think of lemon trees now, of flowering cherry trees, of Viennese music? Why here in this place, Aunt Eloisa, do I remember those things? Forgive me. I find myself among prisoners and I remember that in my childhood, when we saw them going by, you told me those were "bad men." I should remember other evils, Aunt Eloisa. For example, Don Gregorio, the judge. His house beside the church. He didn't have a concubine, something rare among his kind. His door is always closed, like a monastery of solitary monks. His Doberman at the gate. This kept the beggars away. Don Gregorio, the judge, reticent, gentle, his smile fades like that sleepy-time music reminiscent of the funeral jazz sung by Mississippi blacks. He doesn't drink on credit. A good Christian, because he is saintly and pious, he doesn't want to know about prisons. Yet every day he hands down sentences of many years, almost without listening to the defense. His mind is made up. When he is at his desk, speaking by telephone to some powerful man who calls, he barely picks up his pencil and writes: "What is the man's name?" "Are the prisoners about to arrive?" Then one hears: "Of course, of course, my General." "I will see to it, Don! And remember me to His Excellency!" He would hang up then. He continued to be Don Gregorio. The lawyers kept up their demands. It didn't matter. People got accustomed to the "Don" of Don Gregorio. And to the daily hangings at that prison.

"Look here, defendant: tell the truth! They found that grenade on you!"

"Grenade . . . ? I was in my cell that day!"

"Yes . . . a grenade! Yes, that grenade!"

The man with the soft voice, the funeral jazz voice, was shouting now. (Be careful, soldier, it could explode!) The Cutting takes the accused's age into consideration. "I sentence him to five years in prison." And that's the end of it. (That little shrieking lawyer should burn in hell.) Don Gregorio.

In the courtroom, flanked by the security detail, I could see the magistrate. He isn't old like Don Gregorio. He is young. He was about to hear my case, and he was more nervous than I was. (Since they'd captured me, on the *Yumero*, on my frustrated journey to Venezuela, suffering and prison had hardened me. In contrast, the judge was nervous.) Seeing him made me think of the fourteen- and fifteen-year-old girls working as prostitutes at the port, brought there from their faraway farmlands to be sold by "Aunt" Caridad, the madam.

The young judge reminded me of that madam's merchandise. He glanced nervously at the file they had fabricated for me. The same method of blame I'd seen applied to the peasants and reservists who had killed Haitians on the border. The invariable method of fabulist judges. My lawyers had been brilliant. Major Ozuna exited the courtroom dejected and with his head hanging after my brave defender's tough interrogation. The judge had decreed a recess. During which, in his anger, he paced this way and that. In his office, one couldn't see a single law book. In that office, he made a telephone call. At the other end of the line someone responded. I thought: "Poor judge, he is terrified." I felt sorry for him.

"But Don! There is no proof . . . !!! It's impossible . . . ! I must set him free . . . !

"All right. . . . Yes. . . . Of course. . . . Forgive me. . . . Don't be angry. . . . I will do your bidding, Your Excellency . . . !"

And he put down the phone. Tired, livid, pensive. A judge of many colors: yellow like the centipede. Olive brown, the color of a cockroach. Almost green. Could he be ill . . . ? The hairpiece was meant to give him an Inquisitor's look, dangerous as a cobra. But suddenly, he seemed ill. He was defeated! "I will do your bidding, Your Excellency." "You had hand grenades on you. . . . FIVE YEARS . . ."

I saw him pick the receiver up again. He spoke with difficulty: "I sentenced the fugitive from the *Yumero* to five years!"

He seemed to collapse. He put down the phone.

.

www.ingramcontent.com/pod-product-compliance
Lightning Source LLC
Chambersburg PA
CBHW041753010726
47507CB00009B/372